BREAK IN

At once guns opened up on him. Bullets plucked at his weaving shape, dug into the clay at his feet, caromed off rocks beyond him. There was more than one man inside the house, he was sure!

He gained the corner of the structure, halted, and considered his best move. The side door would be foolish. They would be expecting that. The same for the entrance at the back. But just this side was a window, evidently opening into the main room where the outlaws gathered.

He'd hung back long enough building tension. Whoever was inside would be anxious, nervously waiting, wondering, not sure where or when to expect him. Moving quietly to the opening, keeping at an angle not to expose himself, the marshal dropped into a crouch. *Then, shoulder foremost, he hurled himself through the window into the shadowy room beyond . . .*

Ⓞ SIGNET BRAND WESTERN

Other SIGNET Westerns You'll Enjoy

The Doomsday Posse

☆ ☆ ☆

by

Ray Hogan

A SIGNET BOOK

NEW AMERICAN LIBRARY

TIMES MIRROR

All of the characters in this book are fictitious,
and any resemblance to actual persons,
living or dead, is purely coincidental.

. . . to my good friend
Gorden E. Morrow

The
Doomsday
Posse

CHAPTER I

John Rye stirred wearily, brushing with the back of a hand at the sweat accumulated on his forehead. He was sprawled along the rim of a box canyon; he had lain there the entire day observing the activities of the outlaw camp some quarter mile below in the distance.

He reckoned he'd learned all that he could expect to from that point. Harry Wilse had a well-organized gang—a dozen or so members whom he recognized, and who were evidently permanent members; another dozen who were probably outsiders hanging around the fringe hoping someday to be taken in as regulars; several slatternly women recruited no doubt from saloons; a Mexican cook; and the cook's elderly husband, who seemed to serve as a general handyman, hostler, and general roustabout.

Harry Wilse—Rye remembered him from Cheyenne and certain other towns in Wyoming, Montana, and the Dakotas. Harry had been small-time then, a two-bit card sharp, grifter, and penny-ante holdup man in and out of many jails. Somewhere along the way he had graduated, turning up next along the New Mexico-Colorado border as leader of a ruthless gang of outlaws who were having things all their way insofar as the law was concerned.

Holed up in an old two-story house, once the property of an Englishman who had dreams of building himself a cattle empire but lost to the invincible forces of drought, blizzard, and abetting rustlers, Wilse and his band preyed at will on the gold and silver shipments coming out of the nearby mountains, the stagecoaches plying the highways, solitary pilgrims, and the banks and merchants of the smaller towns scattered infrequently about in the four state and territory area of New Mexico, Colorado, Texas, and Kansas.

Numerous attempts had been made to bring a halt to the Wilse gang activities, none with any notable amount of success. The impregnability of their hideout, set deep within a high-walled, brush-filled canyon; its proximity to a panhandle stretch of country known variously as Noman's-land, Outlaw Heaven, The Strip, and other graphic names—unclaimed by adjacent organized neighbors and therefore devoid of jurisdiction insofar as the law was concerned—and an excellent communication system that existed between Wilse and certain well-paid outsiders, made apprehension and admitted impossibility.

Even the Army, induced to leave other pressing problems, failed. Marching up the canyon, which cleaved the east side of a towering, ragged formation known as Big Mountain, rifles at ready, they had reached the outlaw camp without firing a shot—or encountering an enemy.

Wilse and his men, somehow forewarned, had simply faded into the brush and disappeared, allowing the men in blue to bypass them, after which they rode the thirty-odd miles to sanctuary in No-man's-land, as was their custom when pressed.

There were only the women, the cook, and the old man waiting at the house to greet the soldiers and taunt them from the safety of the big house, and the young officer in command of the troopers saw no advantage in taking out his frustration on them.

Posses large enough to cope with the gang had also endeavored to come to grips with Harry Wilse and his men, had similarly failed, and the outlaws, gaining confidence from their successes, grew bolder until at last the critical point was reached. The situation was intolerable. Shipments of bullion had come to a standstill; travelers were avoiding the area, and business for merchants in towns within a hundred-mile radius of Big Mountain had fallen off to where many faced bankruptcy.

That was when Special U. S. Marshal John Rye, at that moment in Montana, had been called in, and the job of wiping out the Wilse gang permanently, once and for all, and by whatever means he deemed necessary, was placed on his shoulders.

A cool, utterly ruthless man in his dealings with outlaws, veteran of a half hundred situations of like nature, and thorough in his ways, Rye initially spent time perusing reports of the previous attempts made by the Army, posses, and individual lawmen. Those digested, he had then ridden to Kansas, paused at Dodge City and searched out an old friend, buffalo hunter and scout Jubilee Jensen, who was well acquainted with the Big Mountain area, and had had a lengthy talk with him.

Getting his bearings and considerable advice from Jensen, Rye continued his journey, making his way carefully to the rim above the box canyon for a personal look at the hideout, considered it at length, and formulated his plan. He'd backtracked after that, and gone on to Denver, although there were several settlements much nearer where telegraph service was available. But wary of Wilse's network of informants, the lawman chose to take no chances on his plans or his presence in that part of the country being made known to the outlaws.

He'd sent his requirements to his superior, requesting five top lawmen drawn from the ranks of U. S. marshals and sheriffs, naming three—Joe Dix, T. J. Yocum, and Bob Shuster—as men for whom he had preference, and directed they meet with him on the first day of the coming month, August, on the east side of Capulin Mountain, an extinct volcano some ten miles northwest of the outlaws' hideout. Rye made it plain the lawmen were to use extreme caution in keeping their mission as well as their presence in the area secret. He undertook the task of bringing in Jubilee Jensen as his own.

Five lawmen, a buffalo hunter, and himself to go up against a gang of outlaws three, perhaps four times as large? Forces in the past much greater in number had tried and failed; thus it was only natural that the number of men specified be questioned—but knowing John Rye, it was a matter of verifying the accuracy of the telegraph operator rather than challenging Rye's wisdom.

Accordingly, the wheels had been put in motion, and now, one day short of the designated rendezvous date, John Rye was having his last look at the canyon and the camp of Harry Wilse and his followers. Rye had devised a good, workable plan, one based on the outlaws' predilection to fade off into the brush and flee rather than stand and fight; it should succeed.

Drawing back so as to not be silhouetted on the edge of the palisade, Rye pulled himself erect. For a long minute he stood motionless, a tall, well-built man in a flat-crowned hat, leather vest, gray shield shirt, cord pants, and knee high boots.

He was a lethal looking sort of man; he had dark, curling hair; thick, overhanging brows; and cold blue eyes set deep in narrowed lids. A dark crescent of a mustache curved down over a mouth that perhaps was a bit too large for his lean, flat-planed face.

There was a completely controlled way about him, a quiet deliberateness in his manner that bespoke conviction and determination and gave the impression that he knew precisely what he intended to do, and no power on God's earth was going to prevent him from doing so. As could be expected, he was a loner in the true sense of the word; no man or woman had ever succeeded in getting inside the aura of remoteness that clothed him.

Turning, he moved quickly back through the loose rocks and stubby weeds on the surface of the crest to where his horse, a big chestnut gelding, waited. Mounting, he cut down the slope, pointing for distant Capulin Mountain. By morning the men who were to help him would be there; he wanted to be on hand when they arrived.

CHAPTER II

Jubilee Jensen was the first to put in an appearance. Riding a small black mare, he arrived shortly after dawn and halted just outside Rye's camp, where he waited quietly and patiently for a full five minutes before entering.

"You've lived around the Indians for so long you've come to think just like them," Rye said with a grin as he shook the scout's hand.

Jubilee nodded, spat. "Fellow never knows who might be hanging around in the brush," he said. "Just ain't my habit to take no chances."

A small, ruddy-faced man somewhere in his sixties, Jensen was clad in worn deerskins, knee-high moccasins, and an ancient homburg-style hat that had been altered by the addition of earflaps stitched to its brim. He had darting, black eyes, seemingly all-encompassing, a full mustache, and a short beard stained from the cud of tobacco that he shifted constantly from one cheek to the other. He carried no pistol, but had instead a rifle with a full belt of cartridges and a long-bladed knife.

"Reckon I'm the first one on the spot," he said, glancing around.

"You are," Rye stated and pointed at the pot of coffee and spider of fried bacon and potatoes setting over a small fire. "Help yourself."

Jensen, picketing his horse with the lawman's chestnut a few strides from camp, came back, his cowhide footwear making only a soft padding sound as he moved. Squatting by the fire, he scooped out a portion of the food onto a plate provided by Rye, and settled onto his haunches to eat. He asked no questions and made no comments, knowing the lawman would outline his plans when the party was complete.

"John—"

Rye, sitting with his back to a rock, nursing a cup of coffee laced with whiskey from the bottle in his saddlebags, grinned at Jensen. The old man had moments earlier gestured toward the brush below them, indicating the approach of someone.

"Right here," he answered.

It was Joe Dix. About Rye's own age, they had worked together before. Now an Arizona sheriff, he was slim, dark, and noted for his fast gun. He had embellished his ordinary range clothing somewhat with a beaded hatband, belt, and cuffs.

Dix, looking a bit drawn to John Rye, circled the camp with his horse, tied it with the others, and doubled back. Stepping up to the marshal, he shook hands warmly; went through an introduction to Jensen, who commented favorably on the Indian beadwork; and then settled himself on a nearby rock.

"Who else's coming?" he asked.

"I asked for you, Bob Shuster, and T. J. Yocum," Rye replied.

"Good men," Dix said. "They all?"

"Two more," Rye said, eyeing Dix narrowly. There was something on the man's mind, something that was troubling him. "Ain't sure who they'll be, but I asked for the best. Everything going all right for you?"

"Sure, sure," Dix said and shifted his attention to the lower brush, where a rider had broken suddenly into view.

A tall, narrow man on a sorrel, sitting ramrod straight on the saddle, early sunlight glinting off the bandolier of cartridges hanging from a shoulder, moved up to the edge of the small clearing. Nodding crisply, he let his eyes drift over the men at the fire.

"Name's Hugh Gannon. Which one of you's John Rye?" he asked with an unmistakable Texas drawl.

Rye stepped forward. "That's me," he said, offering his hand, and when the greeting was over, stepped back and pointed at the early arrivals. "Fellow there in the deerskins is Jubilee Jensen. Other man's Joe Dix, sheriff from down Arizona way."

Gannon, his carriage Army brass, and more than likely Confederate, bucked his head to each, and swinging wide of the camp, left his sorrel with the other mounts.

"Coffee sure smells good," he commented, returning. "Mind if I help myself?"

"Plenty there. Grub, too, if you're hungry," Rye said. "You ride up from Texas?"

"Fort Worth," Gannon said, filling a tin cup. "Saw a rider behind me. Was a spell ago, but I reckon he'll be pretty close by now. Was forking a blaze-faced bay."

Rye was not one to hazard guesses, but it sounded as if it could be T. J. Yocum. T.J.—the lawman went by the initials, and as far as anyone knew had no given name—owned such a horse.

Rye proved to be correct. A quarter hour later the squat, elderly man wearing his familiar faded tan corduroy suit, flat-heeled boots, and narrow-brimmed hat, customary stogie clenched between his teeth, swung in to the camp and dismounted. Famed in his area for having taken seven hardcase outlaws singlehandedly in a shootout during a bank robbery, he was in appearance the antithesis of a gunslinger-lawman.

Slapping the bay on the rump, he sent it trotting over to join the other horses and stepped up to Rye. "Howdy, John. Mighty glad to see you again—and I'm sure proud you rung me in on this little shindig you're giving."

"Glad you could make it," Rye answered, and introduced him around.

After the spare amenities were concluded, Yocum again turned to Rye. "How many more you got coming?"

"Two. Bob Shuster'll be one."

T.J. considered that thoughtfully and nodded. "Good man. Who's the other'n?"

"Don't know. . . . Plenty of coffee and grub there if you haven't eaten. Cooked up extra this morning, figuring you'd all come in ganted."

Yocum said, "You figured right," and taking a telescoping tin cup from the pocket of his coat, snapped it open and filled it from the coffee pot. Settling back then, he watched as Jubilee added more water to the grounds in the blackened container and strengthened the brew with a generous handful of freshly crushed beans from the sack Rye had left close by.

"Good coffee—strong," Yocum said approvingly when his cup was empty and then proceeded to help himself to the meat and potatoes and a chunk of the bread. The supply in the frying pan was diminishing.

"You reckon I'd best throw a mite more fodder in that spider?" the old scout asked, glancing to Rye.

The lawman gave the idea consideration. "Two more coming. Expect we ought."

It was midmorning when Bob Shuster arrived. A longtime acquaintance of Rye's, he was a smiling, youthful man with a reckless manner. But a deadliness lay deep in his flat, gray eyes, and John Rye could think of few other men he'd prefer to have siding him in a showdown than Bob Shuster.

Picketing the black he was riding, Shuster joined the other men, acknowledging the introductions with a slow, cool smile, after which he filled the cup he'd taken from his saddlebags with coffee from the pot. Taking a swallow, he grimaced.

"Good," he said, and laid his glance on Jubilee. "Takes a mountain man to make it right."

Jensen wiped his mouth with the back of a freckled hand. "Always figured if a man wasn't full-growed, the right kind of coffee'd finish the job up for him. John's got some liquor there if you're wanting it flavored."

Shuster wagged his head. "Coffee's coffee, and liquor's liquor. Ain't never been no hand to mix them."

"Where'd you come in from, Shuster?" Gannon asked in his slow, friendly way.

"Kansas. Was working around Ellsworth when they got hold of me. I'm betting you're from Texas."

"You'd sure win—"

"Was down in San Antone a couple, three months ago. John, what've you been doing to keep your hand in?"

Rye glanced at the sun. The morning was growing old, and noon would shortly be on them. The fifth man was late. The hour stated for the meeting on Capulin volcano was early morning, as Rye wanted ample time to go over his plan in detail and be ready to act that night. Irritable, the lawman turned to answer Shuster.

"Put in the last month getting this thing lined up. They had me running down a killer ahead of that. Name was Hazelwood."

"Know him," Yocum said. "He give you much trouble?"

"Only once."

"Good thing," Yocum said. "His kind belongs in the boneyard. This bunch we're going after—I was told Harry Wilse's the head man."

"Wilse?" Gannon echoed in mild surprise. "Last I heard of him he was serving time in Huntsville."

"Ain't many places where he ain't served

time," Shuster said. "Run up against him my-self a couple of times. It a big outfit?"

"Twenty, maybe twenty-four—"

Rye shifted his attention to Joe Dix. The man was sitting apart from the others, taking no hand in the idle talk. Whatever troubled Joe was of a serious nature, and that disturbed John Rye. The hours that lay ahead would be fraught with danger, and a man with his mind clouded by other thoughts would be walking on thin ice—a threat to himself as well as to others who would be depending upon him.

The minutes dragged on. Jensen dozed in the shade of a cedar. Gannon and Yocum fell into a conversation pertaining to the Comanchero activities along the Texas-Mexico border. Shuster busied himself cleaning and testing the action of his pistol, a worn Colt .45. Joe Dix maintained his sullen silence, while back in the brush a gopher barked in its sharp, demanding way, and high overhead in the hot, cloudless sky a broad-tailed hawk soared lazily in circles.

Never a man to work with others except when compelled by necessity, Rye's impatience steadily mounted. He began to consider proceeding without the missing lawman, possibly detained or, for some reason, not coming. One less gun would handicap his plan seriously, but if he had to settle for five, including Jubilee Jensen, then that was the way it would be.

He had intended to use the old buffalo hunter more as a guide and to assist him and Joe Dix at the palisades and not in the capacity of a lawman—but that could be changed. It would call for—

The dry crackle of brush reached John Rye

and brought the others to attention as well. All swung their eyes to the ragged growth below the camp, to the rider emerging from it.

He was a lean, hard-featured man on a husky buckskin. He wore a leather vest, plaid shirt filled at the neck with a red bandanna, and cord pants worn inside his boots, which appeared to have been shined only recently. He carried a bone-handled pistol on each hip, and all the loops of his cartridge belt were filled.

"Pleased to see you're all here," he said in a deep voice as he pulled to a halt at the edge of the camp.

Temper flared through Rye. "You're pleased!" he snapped. "Who the hell do you think you are, anyway?"

"Name's Frank Pace—and there ain't no thinking about it," the rider said. "You're Rye, I take it."

The marshal nodded. "You're late—"

"That so?" Pace said, eyebrows lifting. "Word I got said the morning of August 1. Ain't noon yet, and that makes it still morning."

Rye swore deeply. He could do without the Frank Pace kind, but the man evidently was a top hand; otherwise he wouldn't have been sent to be a member of the posse.

"Picket your horse and get on back here," Rye said curtly, jerking a thumb in the direction of the other animals. "We've got things to talk about."

Pace removed his hat and ran fingers through his thinning hair. "Want to know who I'll be working with first. They all know who I am now, but far as I'm concerned you all are strangers—"

"You'll meet them," Rye cut in coolly. Gone now was the easy camaraderie into which the usually recessive and single-minded lawman had temporarily slipped—thanks to the company of men he respected; he was again tough, inflexible, and all business.

Pace remained motionless while the others studied him quietly, making their assessment and forming their opinions. Then, raking the buckskin lightly with his blunted spurs, Pace crossed over to the horses, swung off, and taking time to have a drink of water from the canteen hanging from his saddle, returned to the camp.

Halting beyond the fire, Pace glanced about. "Be obliged if you'll speak out your names—"

Rye said nothing, waiting while the lawmen and Jubilee Jensen complied. When it was done, Frank Pace brought his palms together and rubbed them briskly.

"Now I reckon we can start this rigamarow. What I want first—"

"What you want don't mean a damn thing to me," Rye cut in icily. "Best we get something straight now, I'm calling the shots—and you're here to do what I tell you, nothing more. Want you to sit down and listen."

Pace's jaw tightened. He glanced around at the other men, a hard smile pulling at his lips. "That there's the fellow they call the doomsday marshal talking," he said dryly. "Reckon I'd best do what he says."

Silence hung heavy over the small clearing where the lawmen had gathered. The gopher off in the weeds among the rocks that littered the foot of the volcanic cone continued to voice his sharp challenge, but the hawk circling above had drifted on.

Frank Pace shrugged. His comment had brought no response. Pivoting on a heel, he strode to where Hugh Gannon was sitting and settled down beside him.

"You're going to have to sort of excuse me, gents," he said, "but I ain't used to taking orders. Usually it's me that heads up these hunting parties."

T. J. Yocum mopped at the sweat on his face and shook his head. "Well, you ain't heading this one—and we'll be mighty obliged if you'll close your trap so we can hear what the marshal's got to say."

"For certain," Bob Shuster added, weapon still in his broad hands. "We know John Rye—leastwise most of us do, and you could be Adam's off-ox far as I'm concerned."

Pace's features stiffened again and a hint of color suffused his cheeks. He pulled off his pinched peak hat and once more ran fingers through his hair, silver in the sunlight.

"Well, boy," he said coldly, "I ain't. I'm Frank Pace, and likely I've killed more men bringing them in than you are years old. Now, I figure that entitles me to a big say-so in a deal like this."

The faintest of smiles cracked John Rye's lips, but it was one devoid of humor. "Best thing you can do, Pace, is climb back on your buckskin and get the hell out of here."

"Now, hold on a minute!" Pace shouted. "Don't go getting all riled up—I was just saying what's true. And I know you've been

picked to deal the cards—I was told that. I just
wanted to make myself plain—"

"Then shut up and let the man talk," Jubilee
said bluntly, and nodded to Rye. "Go ahead,
John. Let's hear what you're aiming to do."

The marshal remained quiet for several moments as if assuring himself that Pace was
through. Then, "Reason we're here's to lay
Harry Wilse and his gang by the heels. Expect
you were all told that."

Gannon bobbed. "What I also heard is that
he's been raising plenty of hell and there ain't
been nobody, not even the Army, able to nail
him."

"You heard right," Rye continued, and gave
a brief account of the outlaw's activities and
the effect they were having on the area. "Far as
we're concerned, we're putting a stop to it."

"Which sure ain't going to be easy," Jensen
said.

Frank Pace stirred indifferently. "Ain't never
yet come across a stinking outlaw I couldn't
outsmart and snap cuffs on."

"Maybe you ain't ever come up against a
bunch like Wilse's—"

"Hell, outlaws are all the same. They just
ain't been going after Wilse and his bunch in
the right way."

Jensen shifted his cud and spat. "All right, I
expect you know what you're yammering
about, but we're wanting to listen to the marshal, not you. . . . Go ahead, John."

Rye smiled at Jubilee's tone. The old scout
was treating Pace as if he were a child.

"There's maybe two dozen men hanging out

with Harry," he said. "About half of them are what you might call his regulars."

"You got any idea who all's there?" Shuster asked.

"Spent a few days up on the canyon rim watching the house where they're holed up. I remember seeing Jack Kincaid and Phin Calloway."

"Now, that's a pair to draw to," Yocum murmured.

"Saw Gabe Taylor and Nate Brown—and a couple of Mex *vaqueros* that go by the names of Lando Mondragon and Juan Berino—"

"Last I heard of them they were in Huntsville," Hugh Gannon said, frowning.

"Been turned loose or else they busted out," Rye said. "Happens I know them from times back. No doubt in my mind who they are."

"Not questioning your word, Marshal," the Texan said hurriedly.

"I know. . . . Got a glimpse of Virgil Fry and Leo McCoy, too. And there's Max Omer and Rafe Dooley, and that young pimple-faced gunslinger they call the Kid—"

"Name's Homer Jones," Gannon volunteered. "Was run out of Fort Worth about a year ago."

"Expect you all know the ones I've called off. They've been around for a long time—in and out of jails and maybe even slipping through your own fingers now and then. But that's not all of Harry's gang. He's got about that many more that I didn't recognize."

"Well, if you didn't know them they must be small-time saloon bums and drifters," Shuster said dryly. "As I recollect, you've got tabs on every outlaw west of the Mississippi that amounts to something."

"Part of the job," Rye said, smiling.

"Can't see where there's any big problem," Frank Pace declared. "Ain't but a dozen or so of them worth bothering with. Why don't we just go after them?"

"It's not that simple. They're holed up in a big two-story house in a box canyon about ten miles from here. Only one way to get to it—from the east side."

"That's where the canyon opens up onto a flat," Jensen explained. "All the rest is high walls, rock, maybe a hundred foot straight up and down."

"The Army tried marching up the slope, thinking to trap Wilse and his bunch in the canyon. Didn't work. Harry seems to have a rule against making a stand. He and his men just slip off into the brush and disappear. When the Army got to the house there was nobody there but the women."

"Women? They got women with them?" Shuster said in a surprised voice. "Sounds like they've set up housekeeping—"

"That's what they've done. Wilse has fixed it so's the place suits him and his doings just right. Hauls in supplies, gets water from a creek close by, keeps plenty of spare horses in the corrals, has a Mexican woman cook and a man to look after yard chores."

"He keep somebody standing watch down at the mouth of the canyon?" Yocum asked.

"Two men—day and night. On top of that, he's got friends scattered around in towns who keep him posted on what's going on. That's the reason I asked you all to be mighty careful and not let anybody know you were in the country."

"Where'd they go when the Army showed up?" Gannon wondered.

"Lit out for the Strip—No-man's-land—it's only about thirty miles from here."

T. J. Yocum took a fresh stogie from the metal case he carried, bit off the closed end, and jammed it into his mouth. "Harry's got things figured down fine as frog hair, seems. He stay in the Strip long?"

"Can't say because I don't know," Rye answered. "Expect he's got a shack over there somewhere that he lays out in until things quiet down for him. Or he could have a friend living around there that puts him up."

"I recollect a shack somebody built over in the brakes along the Texas line," Frank Pace said. "Sets down in a big wash—not too far across the border. Be my guess he'll head for there."

"I'm not aiming to give him the chance to run for it—or any other place this time," Rye said.

"Now, that's the kind of talk I like to hear!" Pace declared heartily. "We move right in, start blasting—"

"And get your fool head shot off," Jubilee said in disgust, "or wind up with a sack full of nothing. Army tried that—had enough soldiers along to eat the place, house, horses, and all—but got outsmarted. We try doing it the way them blue-bellies did and the same thing'll happen. You maybe'll pot a couple of them and they maybe'll pot a couple of us—but Harry and most of the outfit'll slip away and hightail it for No-man's-land laughing fit to bust."

"I doubt that—not if it's done right," Pace countered. "Never yet come up against an outlaw that—"

"How you figuring to do it, Marshal?" Hugh Gannon asked, ignoring the man's comment. "You want to—"

"Hold on one goddamn minute, now!" Pace cut in angrily. "I reckon I've had just as much time rounding up outlaws as Rye there, and that gives me the right to speak my piece."

Gannon and the others settled back and studied Pace with cool eyes. Rye, curbing his temper, waited out the moments.

"It boils down to this," Frank Pace said. "I ain't as impressed as you fellows seem to be by all this doomsday killer marshall business. Expect I can match Rye any day in the week with the hardcases and renegades I've gone after and hauled in—some dead, some alive."

"If that's the case, it's sure funny there ain't none of us ever heard of you," Hugh Gannon drawled.

"Maybe because you wasn't listening at the right time. Now, I know Rye there was picked to head up this here posse, but the way I see it we're all going to be laying our lives on the line and we ought to have the best man in the business calling the shots."

"Meaning you?" Shuster said, dryly.

"Nope, meaning we ought to take a vote on it."

Yocum snorted. "Ain't much use in doing that, friend. I know who'd win out."

"Maybe," Pace said and threw his glance to

the still wordless Joe Dix. "How about you, Sheriff? You ain't saying much. Means you're doing some thinking. Making a choice between me and Rye sound like a good idea to you?"

Dix pulled off his hat and met Pace's drilling eyes straight on. "Go to hell, mister—'cause that's where I'd go for John Rye. Now, if you don't shut up and let him get on with what he's saying, I'm voting to gag and goat-hobble you so's you won't be no bother."

"Amen," Jubilee Jensen said with a deep sigh.

Rye, too, had reached the end of patience. The corners of his jaw showed white, and a hardness had come into his eyes.

"I've put up with your mouth so far because you're a lawman—a good one else you wouldn't have been sent here. But I've had enough. From now on you keep your mouth shut or move on. That clear?"

Pace colored again and his features stiffened. "Sure, Marshal. I'm just aiming to get everything straight, for all of us. You go right ahead, only I'd best make it plain here and now—I'll do the job I was hired to do but don't count on me for nothing more."

"Meaning?"

"Meaning, straight out facts—I don't swallow all that bull about you being so much, and if it comes down to hard rock don't look to me for no kind of a favor. It'll be every man for himself. You stand on that there reputation you've drummed up for yourself and I'll stand on mine. I reckon you can savvy what I'm saying."

Rye shrugged and looked off up the slope.

Jubilee Jensen laughed, nodding to Pace.

"You know something, pardner? I think I'm smelling a mite of jealousy!"

"Jealousy—hell!" Pace exploded. "Ain't no such a goddamn thing! I just want to set things—"

"Shut up, Pace!" John Rye broke in, his voice level and knife-edged. "You've had your say—and we've all listened. Now, you're either going to keep quiet or you're moving on. I'm giving you ten seconds to make your choice."

Frank Pace leaned back and caught his raised knee between his hands. He glanced around at the others, forcing a small smile.

"Reckon I'll stay. You're sure going to be needing all the help you can get. Go ahead and do your talking."

CHAPTER III

Harry Wilse stood at a window of the room he'd chosen for the use of himself and his woman, and stared off toward the flat flowing eastward from the mouth of the canyon.

The time's about come, he thought. He'd made a good thing of his gang and the hideout, but like all good things, it couldn't last. Eventually the goddamn law, or the Army, would break it up for him.

Harry had it figured that way. His many brushes with the law had taught him the inevitability of an eventual accounting—but this time he would be a long step ahead of it; he'd have his pile made, safely tucked away in his pocket—and be long gone before the ax fell. He for sure wasn't going to be a fool again, or be like some of the others he'd known who hadn't known when to quit and were now either dead or rotting away in some stinking penitentiary—no, sir, not him.

And that day was almost at hand. He had

nearly twenty thousand dollars salted away, almost enough to keep him living like a king for the rest of his life. He'd figured he'd best have twenty-five thousand; that had been the amount he'd set his mind on when he got the idea of setting up an organized gang in the old Hudspeth ranchhouse and using it as a base of operations.

It had taken a sight more than he'd planned on, however, to get under way—grub, the usual household supplies, feed for the horses, and cash for the men who rode with him. Like all of their kind—and he'd been the same way once—money ran through their fingers like water poured into a sieve, and since it was only prudent to keep them faithful and dependent on him, Harry saw to it they never had reason to stray—leastwise the ones that mattered.

A couple more jobs and he'd be ready to pull out, however, and then they would be on their own and he'd not have to look out for them. There was that bank in Newton to be taken, for one. His share should be at least three thousand dollars if the reports his scouts had provided him with were true—and he had no reason to doubt them. The two who were keeping him posted, a kid who worked in the bank and fellow that was running a gun shop, were right there where they could see just what was going on. Both had suggested that the holdup take place on a weekend. Deposits were heaviest then, they said.

By the time all the hooraw over that had died off, he would need to start thinking and planning on that gold shipment being moved, secretly, to Denver. There would be about a month's lapse during which it would all work out right.

Thinking of the gold brought a smile to Harry Wilse's lips. Because of him and his activities, the shipment was all hush-hush, but his scouts had turned up word of it—were up there now, in fact, working out the final details with their inside man, a fellow who worked for the mining company. If the figures he'd been given were correct, Harry estimated his share would be around five thousand—and that was after everybody, including the inside man, got his cut.

Harry Wilse reckoned his success was due to the fact that he was not greedy, but always saw to it that those who worked with him got a fair share—and that he had a knack for planning and organizing. He had men—scouts, he liked to call them—scattered throughout the area, all reporting to him regularly and who received a proportionate share of the spoils, as did the men who stood watch at the mouth of the canyon.

He had sufficient followers to never pass up a good thing, dispatching a half dozen or more here, three or four there, perhaps a pair to some other point, it all depending on the nature and importance of the opportunity presented.

He, himself, led the parties that went after the big money, however—not that he didn't trust Kincaid or Phin Calloway and the others who'd been with him from the start—it was simply that, after all, it was his outfit, and he felt it only smart to keep everyone concerned aware of that fact.

Kincaid and the rest respected him for it, although for a slightly different reason. That he was willing to take his chances right along with them stood high in their minds; too, each was comforted and reassured by the knowledge that he would look after them, see to their care if they got themselves shot up, while providing them with a safe place to hide out when and if necessary.

The old Hudspeth house had proved ideal for Wilse's needs. He had taken the best room for himself and Ruby, the women he presently was using as his personal property, and turned the rest into a sort of hotel. Two others in the gang, Rafe Dooley and Virgil Fry, had women friends also, and he permitted them separate quarters.

The remainder of the men shared the rooms left over except for the rear upstairs, where several saloon girls he'd persuaded to move in— Nola, Annie, Bertha, and Lottie—maintained a convenient brothel.

All took their meals at a large table in the kitchen where a Mexican woman did the cooking aided by her husband, who also served as hostler and yardman.

It was a fine setup, and Harry Wilse was proud of it, for by choosing his followers carefully, operating on a hit-and-run basis, and maintaining a kind of neutrality with the merchants in the towns close by, he had succeeded in making outlawry pay off handsomely.

Pleased with his thoughts, Harry turned and walked to the door that let out into the large room that had once been the Hudspeth parlor. It was now a central gathering place where the men spent their spare time playing cards, drinking, and taking their ease. A round of poker was then in progress; they'd all be broke by the time the bank job was due. That's where the difference came—he was hanging onto his cash while all they thought about was swilling rotgut whiskey, gambling, and the women.

Moving through the doorway, Wilse paused. A fairly tall man, handsome by some standards with dark hair, dark eyes, and full mustache, he was a good dresser and took pride in his appearance—now that he had the where-withal to do so. Expert with the pistol he carried and totally cold-blooded in his calculating, he was far from the dandy some, at first glance, might assume.

The card game had been going on throughout the night, with players dropping out periodically while others took their places. Several of the men glanced up as Wilse entered and nodded.

"Morning, boss," one greeted.

It was hawk-faced Nate Brown. Harry said, "Morning. You seen Ruby?"

Nate jerked a thumb at the front door, an ornate bit of oak and squares of colored glass. "Went outside a time ago."

Wilse's jaw tightened. Ruby had pushed him away and crawled out of bed, angry at him for some reason—a remark he'd said in jest to Lottie, the little redhead, he supposed it was. It had meant nothing, but Ruby had made an issue of it.

The hell with her. He wasn't aiming to take her along when he pulled out, anyway. She'd been around for about a year now and he reckoned that was long enough to keep any woman. Besides, Ruby had let herself go; she was no longer the fine looker she'd been when he'd met her. He'd forgotten what town it was, but it was during a bank robbery.

Ruby had been outside the building when he and the boys came out, a tall, full-breasted, well-shaped woman with blond hair and big brown eyes. She'd given him a howdy-friend kind of a smile as he backed toward her, gun in hand, instead of yelling bloody murder like most women caught in the middle of a holdup would do.

He'd grown tired of the girl he was living with at the time, and had turned her out, which put him in the market for a new bed partner, and Ruby not only looked good but also had a willingness in her glance.

"Want to come along?" he'd asked.

She had hesitated only a moment, then replied, "You bet," and followed him to where the horses were waiting. She'd climbed up behind him on the saddle—and that was how it had begun.

To this day he'd learned nothing more about her—her last name, where she came from, or why she had accepted his invitation so readily. He liked to think it was because of his looks and his go-to-hell manner, and he guessed, when it came right down to it, that those really were the reasons.

Someone was slamming around upstairs, and back in the kitchen old Cruzita was rattling pans as she went about getting the morning meal together. Wilse listened to the racket for a brief time, eyes on the yard, which was visible through the front windows. Ruby would be out there sulking, probably telling her so-called troubles to one of the other women. The hell with Ruby.

Pivoting, he started for the kitchen and a morning cup of coffee. . . . Thirty days, more or less, and he'd be out of it. Nobody—nothing was going to prevent his reaching that goal. Wilse paused and glanced at a calendar on the wall. August 1. By the middle of September he'd be far away enjoying a new life—and a new woman.

CHAPTER IV

"You was talking about that box canyon," T. J. Yocum said, puffing on his stogie. "If we can't move in on Wilse and his bunch from the front, and there ain't nothing but palisades in the back and on the sides, how we going to do it?"

"From both—the back and front," Rye said.

Bob Shuster shook his head. "Thought you said them walls was straight up and down—and maybe a hundred foot high?"

"They are—but there's a way to get down using a rope. Jubilee told me how the land lay, so I rode over and spent some time sizing things up. It can be done."

"Who'll be doing it—climbing down a hundred feet of rope?" Pace asked skeptically.

"Me and Joe Dix," the marshal replied. "Won't be that much rope—only about half. There's a ledge we can let ourselves down onto, then hook the rope onto a rock or one of the cedars I saw growing, and go the rest of the way."

31

"Could be you're overlooking a little something," Pace continued. "Just how're you going to get the rope untied from the top so's you can use it the second time?"

"Be easy enough to take two ropes," Rye said, shrugging, "but Jubilee'll be going with us and he'll drop it down to us. Need him there so's he can look after our horses. Can't leave them up there on the rim."

Frank Pace settled back, satisfied. Yocum said, "That put you in behind the house?"

"We'll be a couple a hundred yards back of it when we get down. Should be able to work in closer. Lots of brush and rocks."

"What'll you want us to be doing?" Gannon asked.

"When Joe and Jubilee and me start for the top of the canyon, you'll be spread out across the bottom. First thing you'll have to do is take care of the two men standing watch. You've got to do it quiet. A gunshot or any kind of a ruckus will tip off the bunch at the house.

"Then you move in—get as close to the place as you can and sit tight. Wilse and his bunch all go inside and have breakfast at the same time—that means they'll be bottled up in the house. We wait until they've all gone in—I've watched them do it for several days, and it's always the same—"

"Probably when Harry tells them what they're going to be doing that day," Jensen commented.

"Most likely. . . . When they're all inside, I'll fire a shot—Joe and I'll be as near the back door of the place as we can get—and when you hear it, you all make a run for the front door.

Important thing is we don't do anything until every last one of them is inside. This is one time Harry and his bunch aren't going to duck into the brush and get away.

"It's important, too, that all of you get as close to the house as you can. I don't want any of them getting past you once the shooting starts."

"First thing they'll do is try to get to their horses and run for cover," Jensen said. "And any of them making it'll sure'n hell give us the slip. I've got a hunch there's a couple of side trails out of that canyon. I just don't see how Harry and them could dodge the Army and them posses unless there was."

"There'll be four of us out front," Gannon said. "Expect it'd be smart for us to keep sort of strung out—like a forage line."

"Five of you, counting Jubilee. He'll be back in plenty of time to side you. I couldn't get much of a look at the front of the place, but I figure there's at least two windows and the door. Might be smart for two of you—whichever ones are at the ends of the line—to hold off, watch the sides."

Yocum nodded. "What I was thinking. With you and Dix busting through the back, and three of us coming at them from the front, we ought to be throwing enough lead to tame them down—but there ought to be somebody standing by just in case a couple of strays gets by us."

"One thing we best clear up now, Marshal," Gannon said. "You want them alive and kicking?"

Rye was silent for a time as if weighing the

question and arriving at an answer. Finally, "I reckon that's going to be up to them. Been a rule of mine to always give a man his choice—throw down his gun or use it. Thing to keep in mind, however, is that our job's to put an end to Harry Wilse and his bunch. How it's done is being left up to us."

Yocum glanced toward the horses, stirring about for some reason. "Harry'll fight," he said after a bit. "And so'll all them siding him. Expect every last one of them's looking at ten, fifteen years behind bars, or maybe even a rope, if ever they get caught."

Rye nodded. "That's about the size of it, and you all best keep that in mind, too. Take no chances on any of them."

"You leaving it up to us?" Shuster asked.

"Best way to handle it. You can take yourself prisoners if you like, or you can spare the law time and trouble by settling it right on the spot—every man with Harry is guilty as sin, with him heading the list. And when that part of it's finished, I want everything there—house, sheds, corrals, and all—burned to the ground. I don't want anything left standing when we ride out."

"How about the women?" Joe Dix asked.

Rye turned to the younger lawman. He had chosen Dix to make the climb down the canyon wall with him not only because of their long acquaintance but also because of his age—much below that of the others, accordingly making him less likely to have any problems in making the descent.

"What about them?"

"What you said about the men go for them, too?"

"Why not? A woman with a gun can kill you just as dead, and quick, as a man. If they stay out of the way, leave them be. If they take a hand—shoot them. I don't figure there's any difference when they put themselves on the same level as a man."

Dix nodded slowly. Then, "What happens if they keep out of the shooting and then we burn the place down? Can't just leave them there, stranded."

John Rye shrugged indifferently. "Reckon that'll be their problem, but I expect they'll handle it. They're hardcases, every one of them, else they wouldn't be there in the first place. Don't fret about them—they can take care of themselves. You go softheaded over them, let them flimflam you, and chances are good you'll end up dead."

Dix settled back, apparently satisfied. Jensen, sprawled in the shade, grimaced for some reason, and pulled himself to one elbow. The day's heat was now making itself felt, and there was the shine of sweat on his leathery features.

"Sure would feel better about this here scheme of yours, Marshal, if I was going down that rope with you and Dix. Two of you ain't going to raise much of a ruckus, and if the rest of us don't hit that front door at just the right time—"

"We'll be shooting two guns apiece—and that'll put a lot of lead to flying. And we won't get caught in a bind so long as you all move in quick when you hear me fire the signal shot."

"Reckon we'd all best use double iron, too," Shuster said. "I've got an extra .45 in my saddlebags."

Rye smiled. "Sort of figured that. Never seen the lawman yet that didn't carry a spare weapon."

"Reckon I'll have to settle for my rifle," Jensen said. "Just never was no good with a handgun, anyways."

"Between it and that knife you're carrying I reckon you'll do all right," Rye said. He glanced about at the men. "Any questions?"

Frank Pace leaned forward. "Figuring this here scheme of yours works, and we end up with some prisoners, what'll we do with them?"

"Take them across the line to Trinidad. It's the closest town with a good jail."

Pace wagged his head. "Why not Dodge City? Jail there's the best in this part of the country—and there won't be nobody breaking out."

It was only natural that Pace would object to something and have a countersuggestion, Rye supposed.

"Dodge is a long way from here," he said. "Four, maybe five times as far as Trinidad. And they won't be busting out—I'll see to that."

"If you ask me," T.J. Yocum said dryly, "best thing is to not fool around with prisoners."

"Way I see it, too," Hugh Gannon agreed.

John Rye listened to other similar comments. To the men gathered with him at the foot of the ragged, black cone, an outlaw was nothing more than the name implied—a person living beyond the rules of organized society, making his way at the expense of others, and all too often taking a life in the commission. As such they deserved no consideration. He, as well as his brother lawmen, had no patience for the bleeding hearts who would coddle the criminal as a poor, misunderstood unfortunate trapped by life and supposedly following the only course open to him.

But cold-blooded murder was something to be abhorred both in lawmen and the lawless, and while he maintained a ruthless attitude toward criminals, John Rye would not countenance wanton killing by anyone.

"I'd like for you to remember one thing," he said when the comments had died off. "You're lawmen. You cut a man down only when there's no other answer; otherwise you'll be pulling yourself down to the same level as Harry Wilse and Phin Calloway and the rest of that crowd."

There was a long moment of quiet, and then Frank Pace laughed. "You all hear that? That was the fellow they call the doomsday marshal talking. Why, I can't hardly believe my ears!"

"You heard right," John Rye said in a low, hard-edged voice. "Give the man you're up against his choice. What happens after he makes up his mind is on his own head."

Again there was a silence, broken finally when Hugh Gannon drawled: "I reckon we savvy. Any of them wants to stand and swap lead, we accommodate them."

"I reckon that's the way it's always been, far as a man wearing a badge's concerned," Yocum said. "They get to do the deciding, and if we ain't quicker, well, it's just too wet to plow.... When're we opening this ball?"

"Aim to move in, get set after it's dark," Rye answered. "We'll hit them in the morning while they're eating."

CHAPTER V

"I'm a mite surprised at you taking all that guff from that fellow Pace," Jubilee Jensen said to Rye as he methodically whetted the blade of his knife on a well-worn oilstone procured from his saddlebags.

They were hunched against a large volcanic rock where the thin shade of a cedar offered them partial relief from the hot sun. Elsewhere around the base of the conical formation the other lawmen were whiling away the afternoon hours, cleaning their weapons, repairing neglected pieces of gear, sleeping, and in general taking their ease.

There was no tension, no sign of restlessness or anxiety among them. The fact that they would be up against overwhelming odds and facing death that following morning occupied no part of their thoughts, for there was nothing new in the situation, only different. With the exception of Jubilee Jensen, all were experienced lawmen who had been down the glory road before and had long since, subconsciously. adopted a fatalistic outlook at life. And as to Jensen—scout, buffalo hunter, Indian fighter— no less could be said of him.

Rye's shoulders twitched. "He had a right to be heard."

Jubilee paused and rubbed at his gut. "Was you to ask me, he's boiling plumb over 'cause you was picked to head up this here shindig instead of him. You ever come across him before?"

"He's a stranger to me, but I figure he's all right, else headquarters wouldn't've sent him."

Jensen splattered a clump of nearby snake-weed with tobacco juice. "Well, for my money they could've done better. Now, all the rest seem fit to ride the river with—that Texan, Gannon, and Shuster and T.J. Misdoubt if a fellow could pick better; but that there Pace—"

"Can't judge a man just by looking at him and talking to him for a few minutes—you know that. It's when he's backed into a corner with you and the chips are down that the iron shows—or doesn't."

"Maybe so, but was I you I'd sure not bank much on him. The man's got a powerful lot of pride, and it's been sort of stepped on. He'll get back at you if you give him the chance."

"I'll be watching him," Rye said. Then, "Noticed you didn't mention Joe Dix a minute ago."

The quiet, regular *whisp-whisp-whisp* of steel against the stone in Jensen's hand came to a stop. Again the old scout spat.

"Being a sort of special friend of your'n, I wasn't saying nothing one way or other, but I ain't for certain about him. Reckon from what you told me he's a first-rate lawman, but I'm thinking there's something chawing on him— something mighty bad."

Rye nodded slowly, attention on Dix. Joe was off to one side maintaining the aloofness he had exhibited since arriving. He was now wholly idle, was simply staring off into the hazy distance.

"Something bothering him, all right. It's not like Joe to just set around with his mouth closed tight."

"Well, you best get it straightened out before morning. We're all going to be bucking for the graveyard when we shut down on Harry and his bunch, and somebody mooning and lollygagging along can get the rest of us hurt bad."

Rye brushed away the sweat collected on his forehead. "Whatever it is, it's his business," he said irritably. "I've got no right to pry, but—"

"The hell! This here little shindig you're planning sort of gives you the right."

"I know that, and I was about to say that unless Joe gets whatever it is squared around with himself before morning, I'm going to be forced to cut myself in. We've got too much at stake. I'm hoping, however, he'll talk up on his own, tell me what's ailing him."

Jensen grunted assent, shifted his cud, spat, and resumed honing his knife. "If'n he don't, you're going to have to prod him into it," he said. "This ain't no time for a *kraken* to be hanging around."

Rye frowned. "A what?"

"*Kraken.* My pa was from Norway. Was always scaring us kids when we got lazy and careless with what he called a *kraken*. It's some kind of a fierce varmint that chaws up folks who don't come up to taw and look out for themselves."

John Rye smiled grimly and nodded. "I'll have it out with him. Like I said, I'd rather he'd bring it up on his own, but if he don't, I will. . . . Not sure I've said it yet, Jubilee, but I'm obliged to you for coming when I sent word."

"This here being a lawman party, I been wondering why you did."

"Was what you said about knowing a shortcut trail to the top of the canyon."

"You been up there yourself—"

"Only from the west side, and in daylight. Coming in from the south and at night'll be different. Man could get to wandering around, lose a lot of time—maybe even take a wrong turn and tip off Harry Wilse's pickets, and I didn't want to run that risk."

"Can't fault you for that," Jensen said. "Man's a fool not to button all his buttons when he's messing around with a deal like this'n."

"I need you up there to drop that rope to us and take the horses back, too."

"Sure. Pleases me a lot to give you a hand, John. You know where you'll be going when this little chore's done?"

"No. Probably be word waiting for me in Denver. I was told to report there when I'm through here."

Jensen relieved himself of a stream of brown juice and wagged his head. "Them high-and-mighties just take it for granted that there ain't nothing ever going to happen to you—like maybe you had a bulletproof hide. Don't that ever rile you some?"

"Never gave it any thought. Reckon someday a bullet will come along with my name on it, and that'll be the windup. No sense worrying about it. When it happens, it happens. Where you heading when this is over?"

"Aiming to take me a ride up Dakota way. Ain't been there in a spell, and there's some folks there I'd like to say howdy to. . . . I'm getting a mite hungry. You figure we ought to stir up a mess of vittles for this outfit?"

Rye glanced to the west. The sun was dropping steadily, and night was only a few hours away. "Yeh, I guess we should. It's going to take time to get everybody set after we reach the canyon, so we'll be needing to head out as soon as it's full dark."

"Be slow going," Jensen said, slipping the whetstone into a pocket and sheathing the now razor-sharp knife. "Be needing to move right careful."

"I'll leave it up to you to get us there," Rye said. "You start a fire while I get my sack of grub. Nothing fancy in it, but there's a-plenty."

"That's what'll count," Jubilee said, coming to his feet. "What we'll be eating now's going to have to last a spell. Misdoubt we'll have much time to eat again soon."

CHAPTER VI

There was only a quarter moon, but countless stars littered the sky overhead, laying a pale, silver shine upon the land, and as John Rye and his men drew near Big Mountain, their caution increased.

"Wilse's pickets will be posted just inside the canyon," the marshal warned. "Means we best stay close to the foot of the slope. Brush and rocks along there'll give us good cover."

"You saying Harry keeps guards out day and night?" Bob Shuster said.

"He sure does," Jensen replied before Rye could speak. "Hear they all take a turn at it—and get their share of the haul same as when they're along, even if they stay behind on guard duty."

"Runs the place like a military post," Hugh Gannon observed. "Not hard to see how he's been able to dodge the law for so long."

They rode on, keeping their horses at a slow walk along the base of the mountain. Coyotes

44

barked from the high levels and on distant slopes, and once an owl swished by on broad, set wings as if to have a look at the intruders moving through the half dark. The air was warm, and the hush that blanketed the hills and flats was deep, almost tangible.

Shortly, Rye, at the front of the party, raised a hand and came to a halt. "Mouth of the canyon's just ahead," he murmured. "Don't talk—and watch your horse. Keep him out of the brush so's he won't set up a racket."

The lawman resumed the approach, carefully holding the chestnut as near to the ragged growth as possible and taking full advantage of the shadows cast by the large boulders. The faint smell of smoke was coming downwind to them from the depths of the box, and several times they heard the distinct and unmistakable sound of a horse stamping restlessly. One of the guard's mounts, Rye guessed.

Rye again stopped. Twisting about on the saddle, he faced the man immediately behind him—Frank Pace—and pointed to a dense stand of brush at the edge of a wash.

"Want you here. Rest of the men will be strung out to your left—forming a forage line like Gannon mentioned. Stay put until straight up two o'clock, then start up the canyon—on foot and slow."

"What about the picket?"

"Don't know where you'll find him. About halfway, I expect. Be up to you to spot him, put him out of business if he happens to be in your path—but do it quiet. Could be he'll be farther left. In that case the man next to you will take care of him."

"Who'll that be?" Pace asked.

Rye shifted his glance to the lawman next in line. It was Bob Shuster. "Him," he said, with a jerk of his thumb. "Why? It make a difference?"

"Nope," Pace replied with a shrug and dismounted.

"You've been told how it's to be at the house. With you all moving up at the same time you'll get to the yard together. Won't make any difference, however, if you get held up a bit. You're to keep back in the brush, out of sight until you hear my shot. Expect that'll be around daylight, when Wilse and all of his crowd are inside eating. That clear?"

"Clear," Pace said curtly, and stepped down into the wash.

Rye let his eyes touch the others in the tense quiet. "Same plan goes for all of you. Anybody have a question that needs answering?" he asked at low voice.

There was no response, and they moved on, dropping off Bob Shuster in the darkness of a large boulder, Gannon some ten yards farther behind a clump of cedars, and finally T. J. Yocum in an arroyo fairly close to the south slope of the box canyon.

"I spotted the picket on this side about a quarter mile up," Rye said softly as the lawman took his position. "Pretty sure it'll be you that will run into him. I think Gannon's too far over."

"Leave him to me," Yocum replied.

"Soon as Jubilee gets the rope down to Dix and me he'll come back with the horses and then side in with you."

"Glad to have him—"

"Put me an edge on my blade today," the old scout said in little more than a whisper. "Pleasure me plenty to take care of that siwash of a backshooter—"

"He's all yours. Luck, Marshal."

"Same to you. Expect I don't need to say it, but if you light one of those stogies, the coal's apt to be seen up the canyon, and if the wind changes—"

"Aim to be chewing it, not smoking it," Yocum said, and eased into the arroyo.

Rye nodded, and motioning Jensen into the lead, moved on.

The scout led them in a circle around the towering, dark formation until they were almost to its west side, and then, cutting in between a massive pile of rocks that at some time in the past had come thundering down from the peaks and ledges above, began a slanting ascent for the crest.

They moved slowly, taking great care to make as little noise as possible, but the loose gravel on the narrow trail and the springy, rain-starved growth crowding in from the sides made quiet progress a near impossibility.

They were a considerable distance from the head of the canyon where the house stood, however, and Rye doubted their approach could be heard; but he was wary of Harry Wilse and his efficiency. Rye had spotted no sentries at that end of the canyon and didn't think it likely the outlaw chief would have stationed any there, but he was taking no chances.

The trail was long, steep, and somewhat tortuous in places, switching back and forth and seldom taking a direct route to the top of the mountain. The horses soon began to tire, and finally it became necessary to dismount and lead them.

"Ain't far now," Jensen murmured at that point. "Them big trees you can see up ahead—that there's the top."

A half hour later they halted in a small meadow ringed by pine and fir trees. Men and horses alike were sucking for wind and Joe Dix, hardest pressed of all, found himself a log and sank onto it gratefully.

"Damn glad that's over—"

Jubilee gave him a studied glance. "It's the worst of it. Still maybe a half mile to the rim. Can ride, howsomever, soon's we breathe them horses."

They rested but briefly in the eerie stillness of the mountain and were soon again on the saddle and climbing a long, fire-scarred slope. It was colder at that higher, less protected level, and the breeze was sharp.

"Winter won't be long coming," Jubilee Jensen commented, more to himself than to the two men with him. "Sure got the smell."

Rye remained silent. It was taking more time to reach the crest than he'd anticipated, and he wished now he'd moved out from Capulin Mountain earlier. But he hadn't wanted to risk his party being seen by anyone while they were crossing the long flats lying between the two formations and so had held back until the last possible minute.

"That there's the top—right where them big rocks are—"

Rye grinned slightly at Jensen's most welcome announcement. First light wouldn't break for another three hours or so; there should be ample time to go down the face of the cliff with Joe Dix and get set well before activity in the outlaw camp began.

Jensen pulled his mare to a stop and dropped lightly to the grass-covered ground. Although there was a saddle on the little black, he ignored the stirrups, riding Indian fashion with feet hanging free.

Rye and Dix came off their mounts in the next moment and turned them over to Jensen, who led them with his mare to a close-by pine, where he secured them to its trunk. As he was doing so, Rye shook out the rope he had prepared earlier, and moving up to the rim of the palisade, sought out a convenient, sturdy tree and anchored the hemp to it.

"Can't see no lights down there," Dix said, looking off into the canyon. "Where's the house?"

"Everybody's sleeping, I expect," Rye answered, giving the man a narrow glance. Earlier he had tried to get Joe to open up, unburden himself, and had failed. He'd try again. "House is about a quarter mile from the bottom of the cliff."

"Might've been easier if everybody had come here and we'd all moved in on them while it was still dark—"

Thought of that. Wilse's bunch don't all sleep in the house. Some use the sheds, so we'd still have to wait until they set down to eat so's we could catch them in one bunch—and we've got to block their way out. . . . You got your spare gun and some extra shells?"

Dix slapped at his holster and patted the front of his shirt. "Both my pistols, and a whole box of cartridges."

"Ought to be enough," Rye said, investigating his own gear. "Man could easy lose something coming up that trail if he wasn't careful. Reckon we're ready, Jubilee."

"Then start climbing down," Jensen said at once. "Soon's you're both on the ledge—it ain't too far—give the rope a yank and I'll turn it loose."

Rye stepped to the top of the cliff, and, drawing on his leather gloves, grasped the stout lariat in both hands and started down the brief slant that led to the edge.

"See you below," he murmured.

"For sure," Jensen replied quietly.

Rye lowered himself slowly. He was being careful, hoping to avoid dislodging loose rock that in falling might set up a clatter that could be heard by someone at the house. He was having no great difficulty, however; the face of the cliff gleamed dully but plainly in the silver glow, and except for the complaining of arm muscles unaccustomed to the strain of supporting his weight, the marshal made it to the shelf without incident.

On the ledge, which ran across the palisade like a six-foot-wide collar, the lawman immediately gave the rope a vigorous shake, signaling for Joe Dix to follow, and then searched about for a base to which he could affix the tough hemp for the remainder of the descent.

A short distance to his right, he located a finger of rock thrusting vertically from the ledge. He examined it closely, testing it by throwing his weight against it several times and decided it was solidly buried in the red soil. He turned back then to meet Dix just completing the descent, and again taking the rope in his hands, gave it a sharp jerk.

Only moments later the lariat came whispering through the cool air to drop about him. Gathering it up quickly he crossed to the finger, threw a loop about it, and after making certain there would be no slippage, stepped to the edge of the shelf.

"Not too sure what's below," he said to Dix. "Couldn't tell much about it the other day, but Jubilee said we'd have no trouble."

Dix shrugged. "If you want I'll go first—"

"No, best I do it. If I get in some kind of trouble I'll let you know."

At once Rye began to let himself over the lip. In the first few feet of the drop he hung free in space, legs dangling, held away from the face of the cliff by the bulging shelf. And then shortly he felt his feet strike the sheer, rock surface. The contact spun him about. He swung back inward, came up hard against the wall of granite, and rebounded again.

The impact had all but knocked the breath from his lungs, and sucking hard, he threw his weight to one side, succeeded in squaring himself so that when he swung in once more, he met the wall with his feet and absorbed the shock with bent knees. That checked his pendulum-like motion, and taking advantage of the respite, Rye hurriedly moved on down the rope and reached the base of the palisade.

It had occurred to him that the lariat might

be too short for the final descent, but standing at the head of the long slope that led down to the floor of the canyon, he saw that he need not have worried; there was a good ten feet or so of rope piled about his boots. Stepping clear, the marshal gave the signal to Dix, and then placing his weight upon the dangling lariat to check its erratic swaying and make Dix's descent easier, he waited for the lawman to reach him.

It required only moments, Joe having no problems whatsoever in lowering himself. For a long minute they stood side by side at the top of the slope, staring off through the pale night in the direction of the house. Finally Rye spoke.

"No sign of any pickets watching this end of the canyon. Guess Harry figures nobody'd ever be fool enough to try coming in from the top."

Dix nodded. Rye pointed to a dark band of brush a fair distance down the way. "Let's make it to there. We can sit back then and wait until we can see what's ahead of us."

Rye did not wait for any reply. Bent low, and with Dix crouched an arm's length behind him, he ran quietly from the top of the slope to the hedgelike growth of false sage and rabbit-bush stretching across the canyon. Reaching it, the marshal halted in its deep shadow, and again threw his glance into the direction of the house, still not visible. There was no sign of movement anywhere, and he reckoned there had been no one around to see them.

Dropping to his heels, he faced Dix. Rye's tone was sharp and impatient when he spoke. "We'll be here a spell—and it's time we did some talking. I want to know what's eating on you. I don't fancy going up against Harry Wilse and his gang with a man that's liable to get himself, and me, killed."

CHAPTER VII

This here's going to be my last go-'round, Jubilee Jensen thought as he hunched in the weedy rocks a short distance from Yocum. Jubilee had had the feeling for months—a sort of persistent intuition closely akin to the awareness that comes over a big grizzly when he knows his time is at hand and he need seek out a quiet place to die.

Jubilee didn't know what it was that ailed him. It was like a glowing fire in the middle of his guts, and since nothing seemed to quench it, he'd finally learned to live with it. But that was months ago, and now he knew he was going to die with it.

He had already come to that conclusion when John Rye first talked to him about Harry Wilse and the hideout in the box canyon on Big Mountain, but Jubilee had said nothing about it. *A man never cries, never lies, and never runs from danger;* that was the code of Tall Bull and the Miniconjous with whom he'd lived, and it had become his also.

Besides, John Rye wasn't the sort you unloaded your troubles on or betrayed your weaknesses to—and to Jubilee Jensen whatever it was bringing him down like a shot buffalo amounted to a weakness.

Strong as the north wind, straight as a warrior's lance, true as the sun; that's how the Miniconjous would describe the marshal, and they'd be right. Men didn't come any better than the big, hard-jawed, slate-eyed lawman. He was one of a kind, but for all that, a fellow didn't go bellyaching to him with his problems.

Sure, he'd try to understand, and he'd be sorry and offer to help in any way he could, but it would turn him awkward and closemouthed—and you shouldn't do that to a friend. It was a woman's place to feel sad, have tender thoughts for suffering; a man ignored his friend's pain lest it embarrass him.

Jubilee stirred, seeking comfort from the pain. Whatever it was inside him had claws like a badger along with a fire pan filled with coals that were continually being fanned into red-hot heat. Turning, he looked out over the hushed, silvered land. Just after midnight, he reckoned; they'd be moving up the canyon soon, and then when daylight came, or a bit thereafter, all hell would break loose.

He'd be glad when it was over—not that he didn't enjoy a fracas. His life had been made up of excitement—saloon brawls, narrow escapes from hostile Indians, buffalo stampedes, shootouts, the smell of blood, of gunpowder—of death. . . . Death. He'd been thinking a lot about that of late—something he'd never given much consideration to before. He reckoned it was because his time was short, and the Dakotas were a far piece to the north.

He'd make it, though, despite the fire and the badger in his guts. He aimed to die among the tribe who had become his people, and he wanted to see his woman once more. Star Necklace, she was called in her language. A relative of Chief Standing Bear, he had married her when she was just a slip of a girl, and she'd be waiting for him despite the fact that he hadn't been back in years.

Star Necklace would welcome him and be glad to see him and proudly show off the three sons and a daughter she'd borne him. Hell, they'd be half grown now, and the girl, who was the eldest, could even be married!

Time had gone in a hurry. Seemed like it was only yesterday that he was a young, strong hell-raiser living with Star Necklace in their tipi during the summer months and loafing about with the braves. And then when the great wedges of geese would start south in the fall, setting his feet to itching inside his moccasins, he'd move on, trapping, hunting, maybe working a spell for the Army.

Only yesterday, it seemed—but he reckoned it was a long time ago.

It was like that day at Perryville—a few months earlier in the year, to be sure, but the same half darkness, the same hush, the same feeling in the air. He'd been Captain Hugh Gannon then, C.S.A., and standing now, arms folded across his chest, he was living those taut minutes over again.

General Braxton Bragg, lean, beetle-browed, black-bearded, and mustached, had been his commanding officer as well as his ideal, and he was filled with an overwhelming desire to distinguish himself in the eyes of Bragg and thereby launch himself on an Army career.

The Confederates had been having it all their way, slicing a bloody, rapacious course through Kentucky until Bragg decided to wheel and give battle to a Yankee general named Buell. It was a hand-to-hand encounter, and Buell's forces gave way. Flushed with success, Bragg pressed on—and ran full into Sheridan.

It was there that a battle really got under way, and Hugh Gannon gloried in the thrill of leading his men on charge after charge on emplacements of bluecoat artillery. He still remembered the drifting clouds of heavy smoke, the smell of powder, the continuous rolling thunder of the guns, the shouts of men and crackle of muskets. And he recalled, too, the feeling when he became suddenly aware of Yankees everywhere—Carlin's Brigade, Goodings' troopers, the 5th Wisconsin, the 3rd Ohio—thousands of blue uniforms, flags—but it had not turned him back.

A pocket of artillery on a steep hill was dealing his Confederate companions misery. He rallied his command about him, and they fought their way under murderous fire to it—and captured and silenced it. But he was all but alone when it was done. Two thirds of the men who had gone up the hill with him were dead, and he remembered thinking, as he looked back down the slope—*a hell of a price to pay, but it was worth it*. He'd knocked a hole in Sheridan's line, and the Confederates could pour through the gap.

And then the word had come. Braxton Bragg had ordered a retreat, and the Confederate forces began to fall back, and with them went Hugh Gannon's hope for a military career. It was one of those incomprehensible turns of fate; had not Bragg elected to withdraw, Gannon's accomplishment would have heralded him a hero; as it was, he had merely wasted good men in a rash maneuver that meant nothing.

He had served out the remainder of the war with no particular verve or interest and only because it was not possible to resign honorably. When it was over, he returned to Texas, and like thousands of other men, knocked about at loose ends to finally become a lawman, which afforded him some degree of surcease from the haunting recollections of Perryville.

This could be Perryville all over again, he thought as he stared unseeingly into the stilled night; Perryville, the bloody, stark symbol of personal failure. Only this time he would not be the one upon whose shoulders the weight of command and decision would ride. He would be as one of those men he'd uselessly sacrificed—but in this instance it would not be for nothing. John Rye, unlike Braxton Bragg, would not turn back.

This was the opportunity Frank Pace had long hoped for, the chance to show up John Rye, to prove to the authorities that the so-called doomsday marshal was just a lot of talk.

He'd done every bit as much as Rye during the course of his life as a marshal, only no one had ever given him credit for it. Living at the same time as Rye was a bad break; he'd been completely overshadowed by the man and his exploits which, when you came right down to the nitty-gritty, were little more than what any good lawman did when called upon.

True, the outlaws Pace had handled were of the ordinary run, and the authorities had never put him in charge of a deal such as this one involving a smart-head like Harry Wilse and his gang of killers, but given the chance he could succeed.

And after this day was over, those opportunities would come his way. He'd played second fiddle for the last time; it was only right that he now have his turn at being the country's top lawman—feared, respected, and honored. A man endowed with the necessary ability was entitled to his place in the sun. It was wrong that his light should be forever hidden under a bushel because of John Rye's good fortune in having been the first to draw the attention of those who did the choosing.

But that would be changed. Today was his day, the one that would go down in the records as the time when the so-called doomsday marshal died, accidental victim of a stray bullet, and he, Frank Pace, had stepped forward to take his place.

Old T.J. they were calling him nowadays. Or old man Yocum. He reckoned he was getting up in years, especially to the young bucks, but he sure as hell didn't feel like he was old. He still had his speed and accuracy with a .45, and he could set a saddle all day without it bothering him too much.

Of course, there were plenty of aches and pains; why shouldn't there be? He'd been shot five times, and those old wounds did give him trouble when the weather was bad, but that was no reason to turn a man out to pasture like a worn-out horse—which was what they were trying to do.

Yocum chewed savagely on his stogie for a bit, weathered face gathered into an angry frown. Goddamnit, he'd served his town for twenty years, keeping it clean and safe! But times were changing, they kept telling him. Changing, hell! There were just as many outlaws running loose now as there'd been twenty years ago—and they sure hadn't changed! And they needed him to look after things, him, a man with plenty of experience and savvy—not that young squirt they were asking him to step aside for.

He kept telling them that it would be a mistake. Experience counted for everything in wearing a star, and they ought to be thankful they had a man who'd been through the mill and thus knew what to expect and how to handle it. But they hadn't paid much attention to him, just sort of stood back, smug and patient, as if to humor him.

Well, by God, they'd listen now—and they'd change their thinking. For a top lawman like John Rye to ask for him, actually pick him to be one to side him in wiping out the Wilse gang was proof of his ability. They couldn't dispute that, and when the job was done and he rode back to his town, there probably wouldn't be any more talk of his resigning.

T.J., sitting on the bank of the arroyo to ease the weariness of his back muscles, nodded confidently. He owed plenty to John Rye for giving him this opportunity to show those counter jumpers at home just how good a lawman he still was. It was a favor he'd not soon forget.

Bob Shuster slouched against the rock where he'd been posted and expertly twirled the pistols in his hands. It was a habit of his, born of boredom, and it did much to relieve the tension.

Abruptly he tired of the diversion and holstered his weapons. He wished it was morning when things would start. Waiting around was always the hardest part of any job—but he was glad John Rye had called on him to take part in sending Wilse and his bunch to the boneyard.

Shuster had worked with Rye before, and Shuster was ready to drop whatever he was doing to come when sent for. The kind of jobs the big marshal undertook were the sort that forced a man to be at his best—and that was right up Shuster's alley, using his guns, facing it out with a killer, a showdown—a shootout where only the best man was going to be standing when the smoke cleared.

Fast gun, they called him, and he was proud of it. The only drawback was that folks left him pretty much alone because of the reputation he'd earned, sort of like he had smallpox or something, and that made for a lonely way of life.

Of course, there were those ambitious jaspers

who came along now and then with the fool notion in mind to prove they were faster than he was. They broke the monotony of social isolation, although for only a brief time as, one and all, they had bought themselves some real estate in the boneyard when they'd tried to match his draw.

Shuster reckoned the tally was up to about a dozen now. Funny how hard it was to convince some men that he was practically invincible with a sixgun. There just wasn't anybody better, yet there was always some jaybird wanting to find out—which he always did, the hard way.

But he guessed that was all part of living, came with the business, a fellow might say, and he never complained. His way of life had been thrust upon him by circumstances, and not only had he made the best of it, but he also worked hard at becoming the best in his profession.

Quit? Hang up his guns as a woman friend in whom he'd become interested once suggested? Never—not even if others like him would let him. It was the kind of life he enjoyed—proving he was the best and earning big money in the doing—and as long as there were those willing to pay for his services, he'd go right on accommodating them. What else was he alive for?

"Shuster—"

Hugh Gannon's guarded voice reached him. The sometime lawman, alltime gunslinger drew himself upright.

"Yeh?"

"Two o'clock. We're moving up."

Gannon sounded like he was in the Army, passing along a command.

"Expect I'm ready."

"Tell Pace. Important we all go forward in a line. We've got those sentries to take care of."

Shuster came about and faced his right. "Pace—you hear?" he called in a hoarse whisper.

"I heard," the lawman said, "and I'm starting."

CHAPTER VIII

"My wife's down there—"

At Joe Dix's words, Rye's head came up in surprise. "Wife! Hell, I didn't know you had one."

Dix pulled off his hat and brushed wearily at his eyes. Far back up on the mountain the coyotes were continuing their discordant serenade.

"Yeh. Got married a little more'n a year ago. Her name's Ruby."

The marshal swore quietly. Then, "What in God's name is she doing with Harry Wilse and his crowd?"

"It's what she wants, I reckon."

Rye stirred and shook his head. "I wish to hell you'd told me this at the start—"

"Guess I ought've, and there was a couple of times when I wanted to but I kept trying to make myself believe it didn't matter. Besides, there was always somebody hanging around—and I ain't proud of it."

It was his own fault, Rye knew. When he

noticed that Dix was troubled, he should have pressed for an explanation—not let it ride as he had done. There would have been time to make a change then, take Bob Shuster with him instead. Now it was too late.

"Things happen a man can't sidestep sometimes," the marshal said, his manner easing. There was nothing to do but make the best of it. Perhaps getting Dix to talk might help the situation. "Never figured you for the marrying kind, Joe."

Dix listened to the coyotes for a few moments and shrugged. "Way I seen myself, too. Man wearing a badge ain't got no business hitching up with a woman. Too hard on her, on him, too, but when I met Ruby I reckon I sort of forgot all that.

"She was the finest-looking woman I ever run across. Kind of tall, light hair, big brown eyes, and a skin that was soft as thistledown and the color of cream. Been a long time since I was a wet-nosed kid, but she fair stopped my heart from beating first time I seen her."

"Where was this?"

"Kansas City. I was there delivering a prisoner. Had it in mind to head straight back home when I got him off my hands, but when I seen Ruby—she was waiting tables in a restaurant near the hotel—I changed my mind. She was a woman I just had to have—you know how that is—one of them kind that gets in a man's blood, sets it afire, and won't let him think of nothing else.

"I got myself acquainted with her, and we started seeing each other every chance we got, which was pretty often. Then time come when

I had to head back, and I told her so. When she said she hated to see me go, I up and asked her to marry me.

"Surprised the hell out of me when she said yes, a fine looker like her teaming up with the likes of me, but I reckon she was plenty sick of working in that restaurant and fighting off all the drummers and such that was after her all the time.

"Anyway, we got married and went back to Prescott. I rented a house and we bought some furniture, and things was going along fine except Ruby didn't like me being gone so much. But that's what a man has to do when he's working for the law." Joe Dix paused, and again listened into the night. Then, "I reckon it was mighty hard on her, and if I'd been thinking straight I'd've turned in my badge and got myself some other kind of a job, because she was sure worth it, but it just never come to me."

Close by in the brush a small animal scurried about, setting up a dry rattle. Rye rubbed his palms together thoughtfully.

"Can't see you ever being anything but a lawman."

"Me neither, but I would've given it up in a second if I'd known what it was going to make her do."

"Throw in with Wilse?"

"Yeh, that's what she done. We were over in Kansas. Had to go after a fellow that had busted jail in Yuma. Figured it'd be a nice change for her, taking her along. Wasn't hard to see she was awful tired of Prescott, so I fixed it for us to make the trip by stagecoach.

"Everything was fine. Ruby seemed to enjoy the ride, and when we got to where we was going, Lawrence, she had herself a big time shopping around and buying up some new clothes.

"I got tied up with the law there over the man I was sent to get—seems Kansas had a claim on him, too—and we had to thrash that out. One day when I was over in Topeka a gang robbed the bank in Lawrence. Ruby happened to be close by when the bunch came out—"

"Harry Wilse?"

"Yeh, him. He seen Ruby standing there, and from what folks told me when I got back that next day, he just grabbed her and loaded her up on his horse and rode off."

"Kidnaped—"

"What it was. I started in looking for Wilse and his bunch right off. Was able to trace them west 'til they got to Colorado, then lost them. Didn't know about this place he had here. I can see that's why they dropped out of sight.

"I spent a couple of weeks trying to find Ruby, then headed back to Prescott—just wasn't nothing else to do. Then about a month later I got a letter from her. Said she was happy and all right and for me not to worry none about her. Said she liked where she was and what she was doing and that she just wasn't cut out to be a lawman's wife. Ended up telling me I was to forget all about her."

Joe Dix hesitated and shrugged helplessly. "That was about six months ago, and I sure ain't been able to do that yet."

"Takes time," Rye said sympathetically, "but

you can do it. Things like that happen to a man, but he's got to go on living. He can't just lay down and die."

"Sort of feel like that's the answer now and then—'specially at night when things get all quiet and I start thinking about her and remembering the way she looked at me and the smell of her hair and the feel of her against me when I held her tight."

Dix fell silent, face tipped down, his shoulders sagging. "Might've been different if we could've had us a couple of kids. She maybe wouldn't've got so lonesome when I was away, and looking after them would've kept her busy. Never could have any, though. The doc said there was something wrong with her."

Rye drew out his watch, consulted its figures and scrolled hands, and replaced it in his pocket. Dix seemed to be in worse spirits from talking, rather than better.

"Could be she's not down there," Rye said, hopeful of striking a spark of encouragement. "Could be she's left Harry—you think of that?"

Dix stirred. "Ruby's there, all right."

"You can't be sure. She pulled out on you, she could do the same to him."

"Maybe, but knowing her, I won't bank on it. She made her choice, and sorry or not, she'll stick with it unless something that looks better comes along. That's what she done with me, and I doubt she's reached that point yet with Wilse—getting tired of him, I mean. Ain't been time enough."

Rye gave that thought. "You're afraid she

might get hurt when we move in—is that what's bothering you?"

Joe Dix nodded. "I can't let nothing happen to her, Marshal—I sure can't. Makes no difference what she's done, she's still my wife and I want her back."

"No way of giving you any guarantees, Joe—"

"I know that, and I ain't looking for one. I'm just hoping—and praying—"

"And that's wrong. It's dangerous for you and all the rest of us. You go down there with her on your mind, being cautious, afraid to use your guns—and you'll likely get yourself killed. You know how these things go. You've been through them before—men shooting at everything that moves while trying to stay alive themselves. I'm sorry, but—"

"I'm not asking any favors—I just want you to understand and maybe be a mite careful—you and the others—"

"No way of doing that, and I think it'll be best if you stay here and keep out of it altogether."

"I can't do that. I aim to hold up my end—and I'm hoping to be the first one that spots Harry Wilse. I'm going to kill him, John—shoot him down for what he's done to me."

"He's all yours if you can get to him," Rye said and glanced to the east. First light was beginning to show, and the land below was now taking on form and substance, making it possible to see what lay before them.

"Got to move in closer," he said, coming to his feet. "Want to get where I can see the house. . . . Only one thing I can say to you, Joe: You don't belong here, not bothered the way you are, but it's too late to do anything about it, so watch yourself. Let's go."

CHAPTER IX

Hunched low, Rye and Joe Dix moved down the slope, keeping behind the scattered rocks and clumps of currant and oak that offered a screen for their approach. The weak gray flare above the eastern horizon was hardening steadily into a solid pearl, and now there was the smell of wood smoke in the air.

"Cook's up early," Rye commented. "Wilse must be figuring to ride out this morning."

Dix said nothing and they pressed on, still unable to see the house or any of the sheds and corrals complementing it. Shortly they came to a rise. The marshal stopped and lifted a cautioning hand.

"This ought to be it," he said, and pulling off his hat, dropped to hands and knees and worked his way to the top of the roll. A moment later he glanced at Dix and nodded in satisfaction.

Fifty yards below in the canyon was the outlaw camp. A thin streamer of blue smoke was coming from one of the house's two chimneys, and lamplight laid yellow squares against the windows of the lower floor.

Men, indefinite in the murk, were moving about the yard and in the corrals where horses were being bitted and saddled. Several mounts, ready to ride, were standing at hitchracks along the side and near the front of the structure.

"You aim to give them their chance to throw down their guns?" Dix asked, crouching beside the lawman.

Rye swore silently. Joe was not concerned with the outlaws being accorded an even break; he was worrying about the possibility of his wife getting hurt.

"They'll get it," the marshal snapped.

He was studying the house, the small yard along the edge of which brush and weeds grew thick, the arrangement of the corrals and sheds, fixing it all firmly in his mind. He and Dix would need to move fast and quietly. When everyone was inside they'd go down the slope. He'd fire his gun as a signal to the others when he reached the landing at the back door. That should allow Jensen and the lawmen, waiting in the fringe of growth encircling the yard, time enough to cross over and rush into the house by its front entrance at the same moment, more or less, that he and Dix would be coming through the rear.

Timing was all-important; they must move in as near simultaneously as possible in order to prevent any of the outlaws from escaping through the side door and windows, reach the horses close by, and duck into the heavy brush, intentionally permitted to grow near the house.

"There's Ruby—"

Dix's voice was strained, unnatural. Rye shifted his eyes to the north side of the house. Two women had stepped into the open.

"One in the blue dress—that's her."

She was tall and well built, Rye saw, but even in the strengthening light he could determine little else. The second woman—heavy-set, dark hair loose and hanging down her back, paused when they were midway across the hardpack and called something to one of the men in the corral. He shouted a reply, laughed, and the women continued toward a small shed set off to one side.

"Ruby ain't changed much," Dix murmured absently when the women had disappeared into the structure.

Rye considered the man narrowly. Rye was rapidly coming to a decision; he'd use Joe Dix, but he'd not depend on him. The lawman was in such a disturbed, upset state of mind that to rely on him would be a mistake—probably a fatal one. Rye would have to go through the back door alone and trust that Gannon and the others, now waiting in the brush for his signal, would be entering the front exactly as planned and thus take some of the heat off him.

One of the horses in the main corral began to pitch and fight the man endeavoring to get his gear in place. Yells went up, interspersed with shouts of advice and encouragement. Ruby and her dark-haired companion reappeared, hurrying to watch and add their comments.

The light was strong now, and Rye had a better look at Ruby. Although the distance was too far for an exacting appraisal, he could see that she was an attractive woman, albeit somewhat drawn and worn-looking. That was to be expected, he supposed: An outlaw's wife, or woman, living in enforced seclusion, denied access to a town with its stores where the essentials required to maintain or improve her appearance were available, could not hope to ever be at her best.

It was a hard, rough way to live, and Rye had to wonder if Ruby, now that she had tasted the other side of the apple, would not be willing, even anxious to return to the prosaic life she had abandoned.

Most of the outlaws, their saddling-up chores finished, and clearly visible and identifiable, were beginning to drift toward the house. At least twenty horses, ready to ride, were at the hitchracks. Evidently Harry Wilse had an important job in tap.

"Ruby's tired—worn out. I can see that," Joe Dix said, his voice heavy. "Awful hard on her—living like that."

The women had joined with the men stringing out across the yard as they headed for the house. The dark woman was laughing, joking, and was the recipient of several good-natured slaps on her ample buttocks, but no such liberties were being taken with Ruby. It was clear that she was the property of the boss, and a strict hands-off policy was being observed.

"Man walking next to her is Phin Calloway," Rye said. "Two back of them are Rafe Dooley and Max Omer."

"You know them all?" Dix asked, interest in his wife wavering momentarily.

"Just about. . . . That's Virge Fry wearing

that old Union kepi. Can spot those *vaqueros* easy. Tall one's Mondragon, other's Juan Berino. If you ever go up against either of them, watch out for a knife. They sliced up a cattleman down in El Paso about a year ago. He took their guns off them, figured he had them disarmed. Berino pulled a knife from his collar. Carries it in a leather sheath hung around his neck. Mondragon's got his inside his shirt."

Dix's mind seemed now to have set the problem of Ruby aside and was thinking along lines that pertained to their reason for being there. Aware of this, Rye continued hurriedly.

"You heard us talking about the Kid—I forget what they said his name is. Well, he's the skinny, cotton-top with the hat hanging down his back. Leo McCoy is the one walking with him. Leo's got a brother they call Kansas, but I don't see him in that bunch."

"Reckon Wilse is inside," Joe said, interest again shifting. "I know him when I see him—and time I'm done with him, he'll know me."

Rye shrugged. It was hopeless; he'd best stay with his decision to not count Dix in on anything critical.

"Can't blame you for feeling the way you do," he said, "but don't let it slow your hand. That bunch down there are all killers."

"Don't worry none about me," Dix replied. "I know what I'm doing. Ain't we about ready to move in?"

The first hint of dawn was now coloring the sky with streaks of yellow and orange, and overhead, crows were straggling noisily toward the higher hills. Jubilee Jensen and the other lawmen would have been in place long since, and awaiting his signal. There had been no shots fired down in the canyon earlier, which indicated they had been able to dispose of the sentries with no difficulty.

"I want Wilse's whole bunch inside first," Rye said.

An elderly man, shambling on bowed legs, came from the side door of the house, a water bucket in each hand. He crossed the hardpack to the well, filled the containers, and returned. The number of crows streaming across the sky increased, and from the trees beyond the sheds a kingbird whistled in its sharp, impertinent way.

The last of the outlaws came from the corral, leading their horses as they angled across the yard for a hitchrack near the front of the house.

"Once they're inside and have had time to sit down, we'll move," Rye said, pulling back from the crest of the rise. "I'll make for the door. I want you to get to that shed near the corner of the corral—"

Dix, also drawing away from the rise, frowned. "I thought the plan was for us both to go in, shooting—"

"I've changed it," Rye said, in a flat, uncompromising voice as he checked his pistols. "You'll be better off out—"

A sudden crackle of gunshots coming from the brush just north of the house cut into the marshal's words, bringing an oath to his lips. Somebody—one of the lawmen—had not waited for the signal.

CHAPTER X

Harry Wilse, in his customary chair at the head of the table, leaned back. Taking up his mug of coffee, he glanced about. Old Cruzita and her husband, Polo, had already brought in the platters of steak and potatoes, fried beans and baked chili, stacks of tortillas, and pots of honey, and the men, the job of saddling up for the day's ride finished, were filing in to take their places at the long board.

Sipping at the heavy, thick brew—old Cruzita would never learn to make coffee, not if she lived to be a hundred—he watched Ruby enter the room, move along the wall opposite, circle behind him, and take her chair on his right. He'd patched things up with her the previous night, and now she was all smiles and happiness, but he could expect her to sour down again when he told her she'd not be going to Newton with him and the boys.

"Aim to be gone a few days," he said. Might as well get it over with.

The clatter of tinware was so loud that she missed his words. Frowning, she leaned forward.

"What?"

"Said I'd be gone a spell—"

His meaning reached her. She drew back stiffly, her lips compressed. "I thought I was going along with you to Newton."

"Who said anything about Newton?"

"You're not fooling me. I know that's where you're going."

"Yeh, guess it is. I want to put in some time hanging around the town, looking things over. I don't want something going wrong."

"I could wait at the edge of town. Probably be a hotel—"

Wilse dismissed the suggestion with a shake of his head and let his eyes run the table impatiently. . . . Swinner, Hank Malick, Bud Everett, and Tom Johnson were late. He'd put the word out the day before that he wanted everybody on time for breakfast, that he had talking to do.

"Where the hell's Malick and them?"

Rafe Dooley, sitting to his left, paused, cheeks bulging with a mouthful of meat. "Doing some trading—out in the corral. Him and Tom's swapping saddles and—"

Wilse turned away without waiting for the remainder of the explanation. All four of them knew they were supposed to be there, that there were important things to be discussed—there was no damned reason for them not being on time.

By God, he'd teach them! He'd let them know that things ran according to plan in his outfit. He'd send Tom Johnson and Everett into Larkspur in the wagon for the supplies Cruzita was hollering for, and Swinner and Malick could take a ride over to that rancher—Hagerman—and bring back a couple of steers. They were getting low on meat, too, the old woman claimed.

Nobody liked being saddled with either one of the chores, the trip to Larkspur always being hot and dusty, and that of hazing a couple of contrary steers across the mountain being one to try the patience of Job.

The crew was about finished with their meal. He'd best get to it. Rising, Wilse took his spoon and rapped vigorously on the rim of his tin plate for silence. Gradually the hubbub died.

"I've decided we—some of us, anyway—will be going to Newton, and not waiting like I first figured. If things look right we'll clean out that bank while we're there."

Phin Calloway turned half about on his chair. A Texan, he had a slow, dragging way of speaking.

"What're you changing it for? Thought we was holding off 'til they had more cash on hand."

Wilse frowned, nettled at being questioned. "Been mulling it around in my head," he said stiffly. "Too many people'll be in town on a weekend—and I got the feeling there ain't much more cash in the bank then than there'll be any other time."

"A feeling—that all you got?" someone down the table—Omer, Harry believed it was—asked.

Anger rocked through Wilse. Goddamn their

ungrateful hides to hell! Here he'd set up the whole outfit, made it soft for them, put money in their pockets, furnished a safe place for them to hide out, fixed it so's they were living high on the hog—better than any of them ever had hope of doing—and now they had the gall to question him!

"A feeling's all I need!" Wilse snapped. "It's all I've ever needed. It's been enough up to now, and it'll be plenty from here on—and any man setting at my table that don't think so best pull out right now. Goddamn gang's getting too big, anyway."

Calloway grinned. "Now don't get all riled up, Harry," he drawled. "Ain't none of us of a mind to go against you. Just that we're wondering why you're changing the scheme."

"Well, you know now," Wilse said coldly. "We'll head out for Newton this morning—pack your own grub and blanket. Want you and about ten of the boys with me. Got some chores for them that ain't found time to be here for the meeting. Ones that won't be going to Newton I want to take a run over to Cimarron, see how things look around there. Like to know if there's anything worth bothering with."

Wilse resumed his chair and beckoned to old Polo for a refill of his cup. When the aged Mexican had complied and was responding to other requests along the table for coffee, Harry shifted his attention to Ruby. Sulking, face tipped down, she was fingering the trim on the front of her dress.

"You want you can ride over to Larkspur with Bud and Tom. I'm sending them after supplies."

Ruby grimaced and sniffed, as he expected. Larkspur was a bumpy twenty-mile ride each way—and the place could hardly be called a town. A saloon, a general store, and a livery stable was all it amounted too—but it was safe insofar as prying lawmen were concerned. Folks living there, appreciative of the cash business transactions coming their way regularly, never heard of Harry Wilse and his outlaw gang when asked.

"Be better off going to Cimarron," she said, petulantly.

"Maybe so, but it's a hell of a lot farther than Larkspur, and you ain't never been much to fork a horse."

"I know—"

Ruby's dispirited reply was hardly audible in the clatter of tinware and rumble of voices that again filled the room.

"Tell you what," Wilse said, suddenly feeling generous, "I'm aiming to go up to Denver in a couple of weeks, and you can come along. We can catch the stage at Trinidad, make the trip in style—just you and me. How's that sound to you?"

Ruby brightened at once. "It would be wonderful! Denver—oh, it'd be so good to see a big town again—the stores—people—clothes—"

"That's what we'll plan on doing then," Wilse said, firmly. The idea had come to him suddenly—and it was a smart one. Nobody would pay any attention to a man and his wife looking around, seeing the sights, and certainly they'd never suspect he was rechecking the lay of the land in preparation for a holdup.

"Best we keep this to ourselves," Harry said,

leaning close to Ruby so as not to be overheard.
"The other women learning about it, they'll be
hollering to go along, too. I want this to be just
me and you."

Ruby was happy once again, and without her
sniveling and plaguing him with a glum face,
he could set his mind to thinking about what
lay ahead. The bank at Newton, and then the
gold shipment that would be going to Denver
next month—they must be his chief concerns
now, and he wanted to get everything worked
out to the last details; it was the loose ends that
could trip up a man.

Cimarron . . . well, maybe the town would
be worth considering, but it had always been
his policy to never pull off a raid of any sort
close to home. Sending the men there who
wouldn't be making the ride to Newton was
really more for the purpose of keeping them
busy than scouting holdup possibilities. Hanging around the place with nothing to do, drinking, they always got to quarreling over
something or other—usually the women—and
wound up brawling. What was that old saw his
pa tried beating into his head when he was a
kid? *An idle mind is the devil's . . .*

Gunshots flatted hollowly in the yard fronting the house, setting up a chain of rebounding
echoes. Startled, Wilse sprang to his feet, disbe-
lief blanking his features as the room abruptly
was a confusion of overturning chairs, shouts,
and thudding boots. How the hell could somebody have gotten past the sentries—reached the
house?

Jerking away from the table, Wilse spun and
started for the door. Men were hurrying by

him, some rushing for the front entrance, some heading for the back, others the side door—even the windows. Panicking, they sought to escape from what appeared to be a trap and reach the safety of the brush. Even the women were caught up in the scramble.

"Hold it!" he shouted, trying to halt the mad exodus. This was one time they should not seek safety in flight—as had heretofore been the rule; this time it would be wiser to stay inside the house, barricade, and shoot it out. "Hold it!"

But there was no stemming the rush.

CHAPTER XI

Grim-faced, John Rye topped the rise and paused. He couldn't tell who had done the shooting or exactly where it had taken place. It seemed to have been at the north end of the yard. Suddenly another quick exchange shattered the morning. Two of the outlaws who had been leading horses around to the hitchrack in front of the house staggered into view and fell.

In the next moment, men and women both were pouring out of the structure, some coming from the back door, others appearing at its forward corners, having evidently used the front, a few departing by the side exit, all dead set on getting out of the house and finding safety in the brush.

"Ruby!"

The name was a cry of anguish bursting from the throat of Joe Dix. It rose above the crackle of gunshots now erupting on the far side of the two-story structure where the lawmen were beginning to take a hand.

Rye swore as Dix lunged by and started down the slope for the yard. Opening up on the outlaws, now throwing themselves onto their horses and wheeling off into the dense growth, he followed.

"Shoot!" he yelled at Dix, but the man seemed interested only in reaching the women, gathering in a group near the corral, and was making no use of his weapon.

"Shoot!" Rye shouted again as he raced for the back of the house, but Dix either failed to hear or was ignoring the warning.

Bullets began to dig into the flinty soil around Rye's feet, whipping past him dangerously close as the outlaws returned his fire. He was bent low, triggering both pistols as he zigzagged down the grade. Three of Wilse's men were down near one of the hitchracks where the horses had been waiting, and the two who had dropped at the start still lay where they had fallen.

He saw Dix stumble, catch himself, hurry on, and gain safety behind a shed. The lawman was hit—just how bad it was impossible to tell. The outlaws were wheeling away now, spurring off the brush. Through the pall of yellow dust and gunsmoke Rye caught fleeting glimpses of Jack Kincaid, the two *vaqueros*, and the sallow-faced Kid. All had twisted about as they raced off, snapping shots at him.

He could still hear gunfire on the opposite side of the house, but it seemed to be getting farther away. Gannon, Yocum, and the others were supposed to close in; what the hell were they doing? And who had jumped the signal and started shooting too soon? Whoever it was had ruined what had been a neat trap—one in which the entire Wilse gang could have been taken.

Rye gained the back of the house, paused to reload, and threw a glance at Dix. Joe was leaning against the old shed, one arm hanging limp at his side. A dozen yards away Ruby, still with the other women, was staring wonderingly in his direction. Evidently she had heard her name called but wasn't sure where the voice had come from or who it belonged to.

Guns filled, Rye crossed swiftly to the corner of the house. The outlaws had all mounted, and most had disappeared into the brush. Rye flung a hurried shot at the few still visible, pivoted, broke clear of the house, and legged it for the shed behind which Dix had taken refuge.

"You hit bad?" Rye asked, as sucking hard for breath, he halted beside the man.

"Arm," Dix mumbled vaguely.

There was a blood smear on the side of his head, too, where a bullet had grazed him. "Was a fool stunt you pulled," the marshal said angrily, peering around the corner of the shed. His plan—a good, simple one—had gone wrong, but there was little sense in thrashing it over now. The damage was done.

"Ruby—she all right?"

Rye drew up suddenly. Three of the outlaws, coming from somewhere on the other side of the house, and bent low on their saddles, were pounding across the yard. He fired quickly at them and saw one wince as a bullet found its mark, but the horse raced on. In the next moment all had been swallowed up by the brush.

"Ruby—what about Ruby?"

"She's still there," the marshal replied impatiently. "By the corral—with the other women."

"She ain't been hurt?"

Again reloading, Rye pulled away from the shed, looking more closely at the women. Immediately there was a spatter of gunshots and the thud of bullets driving into the side of the shed. The marshal jerked back. Not all of the outlaws had gotten away. There was still somebody inside the house—now pinning him and Dix down.

"I asked you: Is Ruby hurt?"

"Saw one of the women on the ground, rest were hunkered about her. Was all I got to see—"

Joe Dix caught at Rye's arm. "You think it was Ruby?"

"Hell, I don't know!" the lawman snapped. "Didn't get a good enough look. . . . I'm going after whoever's inside. I can't afford to get stalled here."

Gunshots were racketing farther down in the canyon, and Rye reckoned the fleeing outlaws and the lawmen were having it out. The firing was not too distant, but it did indicate that Yocum and the others were following Wilse's men, endeavoring to prevent them from reaching the flat and making an escape into No-man's-land.

Again he wondered who had upset the plan. Now, instead of having Harry Wilse and his gang in leg irons, he was faced with tracking them down—and that could take weeks—months, perhaps. And there was a chance some of the outlaws would never be caught.

But there were a half dozen or so sprawled in

the dusty yard who'd not rob a bank again, and there were several inside the house—for reasons unknown. The rule among Wilse's men had always been to seek escape when attacked—get away from the house and duck into the brush as quickly as possible. Such was in accord with what had taken place on previous occasions when other posses, and the Army, had endeavored to corner them; duck and run was the system, and it had always worked.

Not all had adhered to the plan this time. The attack had taken them completely by surprise, and apparently not all had managed to abandon the house. Either they had been unable to get out before all the shooting started, or there was some other reason for staying behind. . . . He hadn't seen Harry Wilse among those scrambling to mount their horses. Could Wilse be inside—alone or possibly with one or two others?

Harry was smart. He could have decided to lie low, let the others take the brunt of the shooting, and then when things quieted down, slip out unnoticed. That would be what you could expect from him. But that was all conjecture. Rye hadn't noticed certain others leaving either, because of the thick dust, smoke, and general confusion.

The shooting down the canyon had dwindled to an occasional report. Rye guessed the lawmen had done what they could to stop the fleeing outlaws who, because of the premature gunplay by someone, had gotten the jump on them. He hoped not too many of them had managed to escape.

"Stay put," he said, nodding to Dix, still

mumbling questions concerning Ruby, and bent low, plunged from behind the shed, and started across the open ground for the rear of the house.

At once guns opened up on him. Bullets plucked at his weaving shape, dug into the clay at his feet, and caromed off rocks beyond him. He grinned tightly. There was more than one man inside the house—three or four at least, that was sure!

He gained the corner of the structure, halted, and again sucking for breath, considered his best move. Going through the side door would be foolish. They would be expecting that—and the same applied to the entrance at the back. But just this side of it was a window. He had seen two of the gang make use of it so it evidently opened into the main room where the outlaws gathered. It was his best bet.

Rye checked his pistols, replacing the spent cartridges. He glanced over his shoulder at Dix. The lawman was still behind the shed. He shifted his attention to the women. They had gotten their wounded member on her feet, and supporting her between them, were moving slowly across the yard for the house. It was not Ruby, he saw. They should be warned, told to stay back, but to yell out to them would betray his position, and the marshal was unwilling to do that.

A burst of gunshots sounded down in the canyon, and he reckoned one of the lawmen had encountered an outlaw, or the opposite. That did mean that some of Wilse's men were still around, had failed to ecape, and that was a good sign.

Rye turned to the window. He'd hung back

long enough, building tension. Whoever was inside would be anxious, nervously waiting, wondering, not sure where or when to expect him. Moving quietly up to the opening, but keeping at an angle so as not to expose himself, the marshal dropped into a crouch. Then, shoulder foremost, he hurled himself through the window into the shadowy room beyond.

There was a scream as the wood splintered and the glass panes shattered. An elderly Mexican woman, standing just inside, stumbled back in alarm, tripped on something, and went down hard. Instantly guns began to hammer. The remnants of the window's upper pane behind Rye, now flat on the floor and rolling frantically for the protection of a thick-legged kitchen table, fell with a loud crash.

Three figures were suddenly before him rushing for the front door—Wilse, Rafe Dooley, and one Rye didn't recognize. Prone, Rye fired hurriedly. Dooley paused, spun half about, a frown on his dark face, and settled slowly. Wilse was already through the doorway, shooting over his shoulder as he fled. The third outlaw slowed and twisted around, apparently electing to stand and fight. Rye dropped him in his tracks with a single shot, and leaping to his feet, lunged forward.

He must stop Wilse before the man could get to a horse. He'd been right, it would seem; Harry, Rafe Dooley, and the unknown man had stayed inside in the belief that the posse, or whoever had launched the attack, would bypass them and pursue the others. It had very nearly worked; only Joe Dix getting himself shot spoiled the scheme.

"*Señor—*"

The marshal whirled. The old man he'd seen carrying water was standing in a back corner of the room. He was holding a leveled shotgun in his veined hands.

Rye shook his head. "Forget it, *viejo*. I'll kill you before you can pull the trigger on that thing—"

The oldster wavered. From the opposite end of the room the Mexican woman called to him, said something in rapid Spanish. The man slowly lowered the shotgun.

Rye gave him no further thought, continued to the doorway, and making no target of himself in the event Wilse was waiting for him to appear, looked out. Harry had not waited. He had reached the horses and was swinging up onto a saddle.

CHAPTER XII

Hugh Gannon, waiting well back in the deep brush that bordered the yard of the outlaw hideout, glanced to his left. Yocum and the old buffalo hunter, Jubilee Jensen, were squatted on their heels no more than twenty feet away where he, taking command without conscious thought, had directed they take positions. To his right at a similar distance was Bob Shuster, and farther over—he couldn't see the man—was Frank Pace.

They were set, ready, needing only the signal from John Rye to move in—Yocum, Shuster, and him charging straight for the front door of the house, Jensen and Pace like the wings of a regiment flung out to cover the flanks of the primary force, poised to close off any attempt by the outlaws to skirt the ends. It was a good battle plan; he'd used it himself many times during—

Gunfire broke out suddenly over where Pace was stationed. Frowning, Gannon heard Yocum swear in surprise, saw Shuster rise from the shadows of the deep shrubbery and move toward the sound. Immediately he followed, angling off to reach the edge of the yard where he might see what was going on. Gaining the fringe, he halted. Pace, for some reason, had opened up on four of the outlaws who were leading their horses across the hardpack. Two of them were down; the remaining pair had wheeled and were running for the brush on the far side of the yard, leaving their shying horses to fend for themselves.

"What the hell's going on?" Jensen, pulling up at his side, demanded.

"Pace—he's jumped the signal," Gannon replied.

"Goddamn him to hell," the old scout muttered angrily, pushing forward. "Might've knowed he'd pull a fool stunt of some kind."

"Whatever," Gannon said hurriedly, "that bunch will be making a run for it now. We've got to stop them—keep them bottled up."

"For certain," Jensen agreed.

Men were coming out of the house hunched low, at a dead run. Some, partly hidden by the house as they had emerged, were already on their horses and gaining the shelter of the brush.

"Jubilee, you and Yocum fall back a bit. Stop any of them trying to get by at your end," Gannon said, "Shuster and me'll block off the other side."

Without waiting to see if the command was being obeyed, Hugh Gannon, in charge, pivoted, and hurried after Shuster. Gannon caught sight of the man a few yards farther on. Shuster was standing at the edge of the brush firing at the scurrying outlaws.

"Come with me!" Gannon shouted, and plunged on, hearing Shuster wheel and cut in behind him.

He couldn't see Pace, but guessed he was somewhere close to the north wall of the canyon. That was good. Stationed there, he'd turn the outlaws in toward center where he and Shuster, backed by Jensen and Yocum, could cut them off.

Abruptly two riders coming from Pace's direction burst out of the brush and bore down on them, guns blazing. Gannon fired from the hip and saw his target sag in the saddle. Shuster had triggered his weapons, too, but he was sinking to his knees, a bloody stain spreading across his chest. Gannon did not pause. At such moments when a man fell beside you, you kept going. It was useless to stop. Shuster was the same as dead, anyway.

A quick thunder of hoofs and loud crashing of brush brought Hugh Gannon about. Four of the outlaws were crossing behind him, lining out down the canyon. Jensen and Yocum would take care of them. Gannon couldn't help. With Shuster down, he had to find Frank Pace, join with him, try to hold a line across the north side.

Guns began to rattle where Jubilee and Yocum could expect to be making their stand. Pace, too, was firing—somewhere to his right. Gannon frowned. What the hell was he doing out of position? Apparently he had given way, fallen back.

"Pace!" he shouted through the filmy dust

and smoke now beginning to hang in the canyon. "Stand firm! We've got to hold this side!"

Gannon rushed on, aware that the shooting now was coming from farther down the canyon. He could hear horses pounding through the brush and an occasional yell, and caught quick glimpses several times of men hunched low over their saddles as they raced across open spaces in the tangled growth. He fired each time, but it was impossible to tell if he'd scored or not.

He was out of it, somehow; he had been left behind. The outlaws had gotten by and were now somewhere below him. Jensen and Yocum, and possibly Pace, were taking the full force of the outlaws' break for freedom and would be needing his help.

Wheeling, Gannon, Captain, C.S.A., again bearing the weight of command and decision as it had been at Perryville, hastened to catch up with his men—his responsibility.

A crumpled figure appeared on his right, bringing a frown to his taut features. . . . Jubilee Jensen—flat on his back, sightless eyes staring up at the sky. There had been five of them. Now two were dead—40 per cent casualties. Too high already.

More gunshots crackled from the depths of a patch of brush and cedar trees. Gannon veered toward that, leaping over the body of an outlaw half hidden by a clump of oak. Maybe the three of them could still turn the outlaws, hold them until Rye and Joe Dix could move up. But first he had to find Yocum and Pace—and consolidate.

CHAPTER XIII

"Wilse!"

Rye shouted the outlaw's name and threw himself off the porch fronting the house. He swore savagely. Ruby and the women were there—caught between him and Wilse. He had to get them out of the line of fire.

"Get down!" he yelled, rolling farther into the yard, but the women seemed paralyzed, unable to move.

The outlaw, low on the saddle, pivoted his horse and snapped a shot at the marshal. The bullet sprayed dust in Rye's face. Cursing, partly blinded, the lawman triggered his weapon. It was a clean miss as Wilse cut sharply around, again reversing himself, and spurred his horse into a dead run across the yard.

At that instant Joe Dix staggered into the open from behind the shed. Wilse, catching motion from the corner of an eye, fired instinctively. Dix staggered and fell.

"Ruby!" he moaned.

The woman, hearing her name called again, whirled, coming about just as John Rye, still trying for a clear shot at Wilse, lunged to his feet. The outlaw, desperate to reach the brush at the edge of the hardpack, twisted on his saddle, snapped a bullet at the marshal, and rushed on.

The lead slug, triggered hastily, was wide of its intended mark. It tore instead into Ruby Dix as she broke away from the huddled group of women and started toward her husband. Impact spun her half about, sent her sprawling to the ground as the shrill screams of her companions sent echoes cutting through the pall of dust and powder smoke.

In that same fragment of time, Rye pivoted. He could hear Joe Dix yelling as he, Rye, raced back across the front of the house, hopeful of intercepting Wilse before the outlaw could reach cover on its far side.

Breathless from his efforts of the last surging moments, Rye came to the lower end of the porch, guns up and ready for quick use. Harry Wilse was just disappearing into the thick brush.

Cursing, Rye emptied both weapons at the outlaw, knowing it was a waste of lead, but easing the soaring anger and frustration that gripped him nevertheless. Wilse had escaped; as far as the lawman was concerned, his plan to put an end to the outlaw and his activities was a total failure.

Reloading, Rye turned and doubled back to the opposite side of the house. There were still three or four horses at the hitchrack—those belonging to Rafe Dooley and the other outlaws who had not made good their escape. He'd take one, ride down the canyon, and join the other lawmen. There was a slim chance that Wilse would encounter one of them—but Rye didn't have much hope.

He reached the yard and halted. Dix had managed to drag himself over to where Ruby lay, and was sitting in the loose dust, the woman's head in his lap. Blood now drenched the lawmen's sleeve.

The other women, features drawn, tear-streaked, were gathered around the one who had been shot at the beginning of the altercation, but now the Mexican cook and her man had come from the house and were also in attendance.

"Goddamn you, Rye—"

At the faltering, harsh words, the marshal pivoted. His jaw hardened as he crossed to where Dix was sitting.

"What's that?"

"You killed her—killed Ruby—"

Rye shook his head. "It was an accident, Joe."

"The hell it was! You murdered Ruby!"

Dix's voice rose to a hysterical pitch. Suddenly the hand caressing the dead woman's face dropped, coming up with the pistol that was laying at his side.

"I'm going to kill you—make you pay—"

The marshal rocked forward. He lashed out with his foot. The toe of his boot struck the forearm of Joe Dix, sending the weapon clutched in the man's fingers skittering off across the hardpack.

"What's the matter with you?" Rye demanded, temper roaring through him.

Sweat was shining on Dix's forehead and cheeks. He brushed at it futilely. "You killed Ruby," he said stubbornly. "You and your wanting to get Harry Wilse—no matter what— even if we had to shoot the women—"

"You're out of your head," Rye cut in. "That wasn't what I said at all."

"And you was aiming to burn the place down—"

"I still am," Rye stated flatly, and wheeled to the women. "Couple of you get over here and take care of this man. Then pack your belongings and be ready to move."

For a few moments he received no response, only blank stares. Finally one of the younger girls frowned.

"Move? Where?"

"I'm putting the torch to this place," Rye said. "There'll be some of my men up here in a bit. They'll be heading for Trinidad after they've set the fires. You can go with them."

"Trinidad," the woman repeated absently, and then shrugged. "Why not? Reckon one town's good as another, and there sure won't be nothing around here." Pausing, she looked out into the yard, pointing at the bodies of the dead outlaws. "What about them? You ain't leaving them just laying there, are you?"

Rye said, "No—and there's a couple more inside." Raising his arm, he motioned to the old man standing beside his thick-set wife. "You— get a shovel and bury them."

The Mexican frowned, looking puzzled. His wife translated the order into Spanish. His shoulders lifted, fell, and turning, he moved off toward one of the sheds at the far side of the yard.

"See that he does it," Rye said then to the women in general. He glanced at Dix, then brought his attention back to the saloon girl who had found her voice. "Man there needs tending to. I asked you before to help him."

"Yeh, I reckon you did," she replied. "But why should we? You come busting in here, shooting up the place, spoiling everything for us. Can't see no reason why we should be doing you, and him, any favors."

"I'll give you one good reason," the marshal said coolly. "If you don't, you can stay here 'til you rot. The choice is up to you."

The woman looked away. After a bit her shoulders stirred. "All right, Mr. John Law, you got all the good cards. When'll them men of yours get here?"

"Hour, more or less," Rye replied. The elderly Mexican had located a long-handled spade and was coming back across the yard. "You best be ready."

"Sure—sure—"

"I ain't forgetting this," Joe Dix muttered in a lost kind of voice, suddenly making himself heard. "You can bet on it. . . . Ruby—she was all I had—ever wanted."

Rye stepped in close to the man and squatted before him. "I'm sorry about her, Joe."

"The hell you are! You ain't never sorry about nothing. I know you—killing's your middle name. Ruby was in your way, and you shot her down."

"That was Harry Wilse's bullet, not mine."

"That's a goddamn lie! You're just trying to

worm out of it. I seen how it was—what happened—and I sure ain't forgetting it! I'm warning you now—I'm going to kill you for what you done to her!"

John Rye choked back his anger and drew himself erect. Dix was out of his head from pain and grief. It was useless to talk to him. Nodding curtly to the women, he spun, stalking across the yard to the hitchrack. Mounting the first horse he came to, he swung about and headed down the canyon.

CHAPTER XIV

Taut, anger again rising within him as he thought of the past few minutes' events, the marshal rode directly down the center of the box canyon, keeping the lean little pinto he'd borrowed from the outlaw hitchrack to a fast walk.

Although he felt Joe Dix's words were products of the man's misfortune, it irked him to think that a friend he held in such respect could turn on him so completely. But that would change, he was certain; Joe would be looking at things differently once his wounds were taken care of and he had calmed down.

But Harry Wilse . . . there had been no shots fired after the outlaw chief had made off into the brush and struck off down the canyon. That could only mean that he had been successful in getting by Yocum and the other lawmen. God-damn whoever it was who had upset his plan to trap the outlaws! It would have all worked out exactly as hoped otherwise.

Shortly Rye rode out of a dense patch of brush into a fairly large clearing. Horses were standing at its lower end, and along the edge of the open ground the bodies of five men had been laid out in an orderly row. Nearby were four prisoners, hands tied behind their backs. The marshal halted abruptly, and then Hugh Gannon and Pace emerged from the wall of shrubbery, pistols in hand.

"Heard you coming," the Texan said. "Wasn't sure who to expect."

Rye studied the tall man for a moment. Then, "Wilse was about five, maybe ten minutes ahead of me—"

"He didn't come by here—leastwise we didn't see or hear him."

"He passed by, all right," the marshal said, glancing around. "Where's the rest of the men?"

"You're looking at what's left, 'cepting for Yocum. He's been shot."

Rye's mouth tightened. "Jubilee? Shuster?"

"Dead. Got hit right off at the start. That bunch was on us almost before we knew what was happening," Gannon said.

Rye swore deeply, riding on in to where the Texan and the totally quiet Frank Pace were standing. Pulling the pinto to a stop, Rye dismounted. Allowing the reins to fall, he turned, looking down at the row of dead outlaws: Lando Mondragon . . . Leo McCoy . . . Gabe Tyler . . . Nate Brown . . . a stranger. . . .

Rye shifted his attention to the prisoners. The blond Kid was the only one he knew. That meant Kincaid, Phin Calloway, the other *vaquero*, Berino, and Max Omer, all old standbys in the gang, had escaped—and would be rejoining Harry Wilse.

The marshal came back around, the same grim set hardening his mouth. "Where's T.J.?"

Gannon jerked a thumb toward a mound of rocks a few strides to his left. Immediately Rye moved past the dead outlaws into the shaded area where the old lawman was sitting. Shoulders braced against a large boulder, T.J. greeted him with a painful smile.

"Them bastards got me when I wasn't looking," he said, and touched a stained bandage encircling his chest.

"It bad?"

"Naw, I've been hurt worse falling off a horse. I'll live. You all right? Right smart of blood on your face and neck."

Rye was unaware of it; he reckoned he'd received the cuts and scratches when he'd thrown himself through the window of the outlaw hideout.

"It's nothing," the marshal said. "Joe got shot up some. Left him back at the house for the women to look after."

He made no further comment on Dix's condition or troubles, but turned away and put his gaze on Jubilee Jensen and Bob Shuster. They had been placed in the shadow of a squat, spreading cedar, their hats over their faces.

"We done the best we could," Hugh Gannon said, as if an explanation were necessary. "We was just outgunned—and they was on horses. Was a bunch of them that got by."

Pace had continued to remain silent during the conversation, seemingly content to let the Texan do the talking. Rye gave that thought, reading meaning into it. Eyes narrowing, he faced the lawman.

"I want to know what happened up there at the yard. Who jumped the gun?"

Gannon only shrugged. T.J. looked off toward the prisoners. Pace said nothing.

"It's no help now, I realize that," Rye added, "but the way I see it, whoever it was not only messed up a sure-fire deal but he also caused Jubilee and Shuster to go down, and got T.J. hurt."

Again there was no answer. Rye settled his cold glare on Pace. "Was it you?"

Frank Pace shrugged. "Well, I guess you could say I sort of started it—but you can't blame me for them getting hit. Like as not it would've happened anyway. We was up against too big a bunch."

"Maybe it would—and maybe not. I'd like to hear why you took it on yourself to start shooting when you knew the plan was to wait for all of them to be inside."

Pace stirred, turned his head aside, and spat. "I thought them four was aiming to pull out," he said.

Rye was hanging tight to his temper. "If they were it'd ben better to let them go," he said, tone heavy with doubt. "We would've had Wilse and all the rest of his bunch then—"

"There's a-plenty of them didn't get away," Pace declared, now showing anger. He pointed to where the dead outlaws lay. "They sure didn't make it—and neither did the Kid and them three others!"

"Not much to show for two damn good men, and for the bullet holes in T.J. and Dix!" the marshal snapped. "I'd like to know what happened to you after you opened up on them four. I never did see you."

"Figured I'd best drop back and side Hugh and the rest—"

"You got a knack for figuring wrong, Pace," Rye said in disgust. "I could've used some help."

"You and Dix get any of them? I heard shooting."

"Rafe Dooley—he was trying to wait me out inside the house, along with Wilse and some other jasper. Harry got away, Rafe and the other one didn't. Was three or four down in the yard. Dix got hit right at the start, else we might've done better."

"I figure we could've done better here, too," Yocum said, shifting uncomfortably, "even with them scattering all over the place. They had us bunched up in the middle. If we'd stayed like Gannon there had put us—"

"Goddamnit!" Pace shouted. "Don't go blaming me for everything going wrong. I done what I thought was right."

A quick retort sprang to John Rye's lips. He let it die. There was nothing to be gained in recrimination. It was possible Frank Pace honestly believed he was right in acting before the signal was given—but that finished him as far as Rye was concerned. If ever again he needed to call for support, he'd make certain Pace would not be one of those sent.

Moving off, he crossed to where Jensen and Bob Shuster lay, and hunching down, lifted the battered old homburg with its improvised ear-flaps and looked down on the scout's weathered features. He noticed then the crusted blood on Jubilee's worn shirt—just below the left arm. The bullet that felled him had entered from the side, probably killing him instantly. Rye replaced the hat. He was glad death had come quickly for his old friend.

He turned to Shuster, and uncovering the man's face, studied it thoughtfully. The lawman's mouth was set to a faint, ironic smile, as if he saw some sort of amusement in the way his life was ending.

Restoring Shuster's hat, John Rye came fully upright. A man ordinarily unaffected by death—an ever-present companion in the profession he pursued—a bitterness was now claiming him. It was at his request that Jubilee Jensen and Bob Shuster had taken part in his plan to end the depredations of Harry Wilse and his gang, and he could not shake the feeling that he was responsible for their deaths. Both were good men—and their dying was a waste.

"I want to say I sure hate it about Jensen and Shuster," Pace began, but Rye cut him short.

"Forget it," he snapped, and wheeled to Hugh Gannon. "Take charge here."

"Now, hold on just a goddamn minute!" Pace shouted angrily. "Seeing as how I'm the senior man, I reckon I ought to be the one put in charge."

Rye considered the man icily. "No thanks. I've had a sample of how you do things—and the cost is too high," he said, and came back to Gannon.

"I want you to take the prisoners to Trinidad," Rye said. "I already made arrangements to have them looked after there by the sheriff."

Gannon nodded. "I recollect you telling us that before. What about the dead ones?"

"Load them on their horses and tote them back to the house. I put a man to doing the burying up there. He can add these to the lot. It'd be a favor if you'll take Jensen and Shuster on to Trinidad, however. I'd like to have them put away proper."

"Yocum ought to be getting to a doc right soon—"

"Closest one'll be Trinidad. Women at the house can fix him up so's he can make it to there. You can bet they've patched plenty of bullet holes, living with Wilse and his bunch long as they have."

"Don't go fretting about me," T.J. said. "Expect I'll live 'til I die."

Rye smiled faintly at the old lawman's dry humor. "I think I mentioned that Joe Dix'd got shot up some, too, and that the women are fixing him up. Could be you'll have a bit of a problem with him."

Gannon frowned. "Problem?"

Rye gave the situation a moment's thought. He would as soon not go into Dix's marital troubles, Gannon would learn about it anyway when he got there; he might as well be told now so that he would be prepared.

"Yeh, Joe's wife was living with that bunch. She was Harry Wilse's woman."

Hugh Gannon's eyes flickered with surprise, but all he said was, "Tough on Dix. You said 'was'—"

"She's dead. Got in the way of a bullet meant

for me. Joe's taking it mighty hard—was out of his head when I rode off."

"Obliged to you for telling me about it," the Texan said. "He bad hurt?"

"Hit twice, maybe three times. Arm and the shoulder, I think. Should be all right if those women doctored him like I told them to."

"The women—what do you want me to do about them?"

"I gave them a choice—help and we'd take them with us to Trinidad, otherwise they could shift for themselves. They picked Trinidad. Let them ride their friends' horses. There'll be plenty extras. Expect you better look after the Mexican woman cook and her husband, too. Can't leave them there.

"Once you're all lined up and ready to go, set the place afire. I want it burned to the ground—house, sheds, corrals, and all. All I expect to see there when it's over is ashes. Wilse and some of his bunch may've got away, but they sure as hell won't ever be starting up again in this canyon—if it happens that I fail to run them down."

Gannon nodded. "Way you've been talking, I take it you won't be along. That mean you're going after Wilse and the others that got away?"

"Soon as you and me've got things understood."

"Reckon we've done that," the Texan said. He paused to listen to the distant moaning of a dove somewhere up in the canyon. "Ain't right sure it's a one-man job going after Harry. He'll have eight or ten of them renegades with him."

"Odds'll be no worse than they were here—"

"I'll side you," Frank Pace volunteered, speaking for the first time in several minutes. "Gannon can look after things here."

"I'll handle it alone," Rye said, his voice again cold and short.

Pace's features again flushed with anger. "Meaning you don't want me along—"

"If you put it that way—yes."

"Damnit, Rye, there ain't no sense you acting this way! I done what I figured was right—and maybe it was a mistake. You going to hold it against me the rest of my life?"

John Rye glanced toward the bodies of Jubilee Jensen and Bob Shuster. "I won't be forgetting they'd maybe be alive right now if you'd done what you'd been told to do."

"You can't say that for sure. It was a fool thing anyway, seven of us taking on that whole gang."

"Seems to me we've done a pretty fair job of breaking up Harry's bunch so far," Gannon drawled.

Pace flung an angry look at the Texan, then swung back to Rye. "The big reason you're wanting to go alone after Wilse is that you're thinking mighty hard about all that glory and what it'll do for that reputation of yours!"

The marshal smiled dryly. "That reputation of mine, as you call it, has been chewing at you ever since we come together. Fact is, it and a nickle will buy me a beer—and it sure has never stopped a bullet. Far as me going after Harry Wilse, I'd be glad to hand the job over to you if I thought you could do it."

"I could, sure as hell—"

"No, I reckon not. You'd make some fool

mistake that'd get you killed—and Harry would get away again."

"You saying I'm not smart enough?" Pace demanded tensely.

Rye nodded slowly. "I'm saying you're not smart enough, and I'm not too sure you're man enough."

Frank Pace drew back stiffly, eyes narrowing. "I don't let nobody talk to me like that," he said in a low voice.

John Rye's level gaze did not waver. "You asked me a question and you got the truth. . . . Now, I don't want trouble with you, Pace, but I'm willing if you push it. Fact is, I don't trust you, and I figure I've got two good reasons, three if you count Yocum, for feeling that way. Let's drop it."

A tight hush had fallen over the clearing. Gannon and T.J. Yocum looked on in silence, knowing it was a matter in which they had no part and were unwelcome to participate. From nearby the prisoners, also quiet, watched and listened with interest.

"All right, we'll let it go," Pace said after a time, "but it ain't over with. I don't let no man push me around like you're doing—this just ain't the place to settle up—"

"If you're of a mind, pull out," Rye suggested, weary of wrangling. "Head on back to wherever you're from. Gannon and Yocum can do what's left to be done."

"Think I'll do just that," Pace snapped, and wheeling angrily, he stalked toward his horse.

Rye turned his attention back to Gannon. "You got everything straight?"

"Sure have," the Texan said. "Reckon we'll see you next in Trinidad."

"Maybe. Give me a week. If I'm not there by then, go on about your business. I'd like to say now I'm obliged to you and T.J. for your help. You'll be getting your pay from headquarters soon as they know the job's been done."

Gannon smiled. "Pleasure was all mine, Marshal," he said in his lazy way. "You'll find your horse back there in the cedars. . . . Good luck."

"Same to you," Rye replied, and nodding to Yocum as well as to Frank Pace halted beside his buckskin, moved on.

CHAPTER XV

Hugh Gannon waited until John Rye had swung onto his gelding and was riding off down the canyon before he shook his head doubtfully. He was wondering if he'd ever see the marshal again. What Rye intended to undertake was a big chore, even for a lawman of his caliber, and he would have been well advised to accept Frank Pace's offer of help, even if he lacked confidence in the man. But it was Rye's decision, and he'd not question it.

Coming about, he faced Yocum. "I'll get the dead ones loaded up," he said in a matter-of-fact voice. "It's a little job the prisoners can do for us. You get yourself ready to ride."

"I'm as ready as I'll ever be, I reckon," T.J. said, and ducked his head at Pace, still standing by his horse. "You calling on him to help?"

"He knows what's to be done," Hugh said indifferently. "I ain't asking him for nothing."

Gannon moved toward the waiting prisoners.

Halting before them, he set his eyes on the first two in the row.

"Stand up—"

The outlaws got to their feet, and stepping in behind them, the Texan freed their hands.

"Load up your friends there," he said, pointing to the dead outlaws. "Hang them across their saddles and tie them down."

"We know what you're wanting done," the older of the pair said gruffly. "We heard the marshal talking."

"Good. Saves me talking—but you best keep this in mind: I'll be standing right behind you with a gun in my hand. If any of you even looks like you're going to try something cute, he'll end up hanging across a saddle too. That clear?"

"The two outlaws nodded sullenly, turned, and paused. Frank Pace had ridden to the picketed horses and was leading them up. Halting near the dead men, he dropped their reins, cut back around, and headed for the remaining horses that would be used for Jensen and Bob Shuster as well as those belonging to Yocum and Gannon.

"He's sure getting real helpful," T.J. commented dryly. "What do you reckon got into him?"

Gannon smiled, said, "Rye," and put his attention back on the prisoners, now hoisting the bodies of their friends and draping them over their saddles.

When they had finished, Gannon secured their hands behind them again and directed the others to rise. Before he could march them to where their horses waited, Pace was bringing the animals to them.

"I'll keep an eye on this bunch," the lawman said briskly. "Best you see to Jensen and Shuster."

Hugh stared at the man briefly, nodded, and cut back to the mound of rocks where Yocum, apparently by great effort, had pulled himself erect. The horses were nearby, thanks once more to Frank Pace, and going first to Jensen, the Texan lifted the slight figure and placed him on the little black mare the scout had been riding and tied him down. He turned then to Shuster. By the time he had him across his hull, Yocum had managed to climb onto his horse, and slumped forward, was waiting.

"You going to be able to make it?" Gannon asked, squinting at the older lawman.

"You're goddamn right," Yocum replied grimly. "I've got to. There's some folks back home I aim to prove something to. Guess I been proving something to myself, too."

Gannon, swinging up onto his horse, grinned knowingly. He'd done a little proving, also—and to himself. He's vowed once never again to assume responsibility for any man's life, but at the critical moment, unable to shirk the sense of duty that possessed him, he had, knowing that unless he did they all would be lost.

Two of his companions had died, just as there had been those at Perryville, but a great truth had dawned upon him: They had fallen not because of him, but because it had been in the scheme of things. Men lived, men died walking, standing, running side by side; who could explain why one fell victim to death and the other did not?

"Move out," he called to Pace, holding the prisoners and the horses bearing the dead outlaws in the center of the clearing. Leaning over, he caught up the reins of Jubilee's mare and Shuster's black. The dark shadows in the corners of his mind were gone now; the past no longer would haunt him.

Yocum, bracing himself with one hand on the horn, guiding his mount with the other, started forward, and Gannon, not too certain of the lawman's ability to stay on the saddle, swung in behind. They entered the clearing, fell into line with the others, and began climbing the canyon's slight grade in double-file rank with Frank Pace alongside, drifting back and forth like an outrider, keeping close watch. The change in the man's attitude was puzzling. Earlier, when T.J. had mentioned it, Gannon had dismissed it with a flippant comment, but he wondered now what was really on the lawman's mind.

It was a slow procession, requiring a long half hour to cover the short distance from the clearing to the house where Harry Wilse and his crowd had established their hideout.

As they rode onto the hardpack, Gannon saw two of the women come out on the porch, and hands on hips, stare resentfully at them. An elderly Mexican man, working with a spade in a shallow wash a bit to the side of the structure, paused to look also. He would be the one John Rye had named as the burial detail.

"Take the bodies over there," Gannon directed, calling to the prisoners leading the horses carrying their onetime partners, and as they obediently veered off, he continued on for the nearest hitchrack.

"Rest of you pull up and set. Pace, I'll be obliged if you'll stand guard over them while I get T.J. inside where those women can go to work on him."

There was no answer, no indication that the lawman had heard. He had been close by only moments earlier. Frowning, Gannon raised himself slightly on his saddle and looked around. Frank Pace had disappeared.

CHAPTER XVI

Wilse and his bunch would head for sanctuary in Noman's-land. Rye was positive of that. They would believe, as had been the way of it in the past, that no lawman would follow them into the area. The marshal smiled tautly. This time they had a surprise coming; this time it would be different.

They had almost a two-hour start on him, and he could believe they all would be riding hard—Phin Calloway and the one who had gotten away first, and then Wilse himself. Harry would be bringing up the rear, a lone rider unless Calloway and the others had spotted him and held back long enough for him to join the main party. It was doubtful that that would happen, however; at such times it was every man for himself, and those left behind did the best they could on their own, but Rye would be able to tell if they had delayed for their chief when he reached the creek some twenty miles ahead.

118

It was typical of John Rye that he had wiped the confrontation with Frank Pace completely from his mind, leaving it devoid of all thoughts but those pertaining to overtaking the outlaws and capturing or shooting it out with them—whichever they chose. Frankly, the marshal preferred the latter; men such as he pursued—outlaws, proven killers of the worst kind, to his way of thinking deserved little if any consideration insofar as due process of law was concerned. By their own actions they had convicted themselves of guilt, time after time; therefore all and any punishment was warranted and just.

But it would be no simple chore, Rye was admitting to himself. He could expect there to be not only Harry Wilse in the party, but also Phin Calloway, the other *vaquero*, Berino, Jack Kincaid, Max Omer, and at least a half dozen others, names unknown but of no less vicious quality. It would have been good to have Bob Shuster at his side, a fast, deadly man with a gun—or Joe Dix.

Rye frowned as his thoughts came to a halt on the latter. Joe had gone loony when Wilse's bullet had killed Ruby, and in his suddenly twisted and confused mind, he had placed the blame for his wife's death on Rye.

Joe would come out of that, though, as soon as he leveled off and got things straight in his head—which was probably by that moment. Wounded, grief-stricken, he'd said things he didn't mean—but he'd be all right. Joe Dix was a good lawman, and it was sad that things had worked out as they had for him. He'd really thought a lot of his wife in spite of the way things had gone.

Hugh Gannon was a man he'd be proud to ride the river with, too. Calm, easygoing, he'd proven himself there in the canyon. The same went for T.J. Yocum, but they were both out of it, in no position to lend him a hand. Gannon had to finish the job they'd started by taking the prisoners and the women on to Trinidad; Yocum, like Dix, was finished for a time.

Frank Pace, had he been like one of them, could have been of use, but Pace had something bothering him besides the chips he carried on his shoulders—and Rye had been a fool to take a chance on him. When it came right down to bedrock, Rye had a feeling that Frank Pace represented a threat, that if ever a moment came when Pace could put a bullet into him or make it possible for someone else to do so, Pace would seize the opportunity.

Why Pace's hatred should run so deep Rye could not understand, but it was there—he was certain of it. It glowed in the depths of his eyes, in the way he spoke, his calumnious tone, in his manner of challenging everything laid out to be done—but he reckoned he'd seen the last of the man now and could forget him. By the time he finished running down Wilse and the other outlaws, come out of it alive, and returned to Trinidad, Pace, Gannon, T.J., and Joe Dix would have gone on to their respective homes.

The faint sparkle of silver in the afternoon sunlight broke through the trees and brush a short distance ahead—the creek. Now he would be able to get an idea of what he was up against.

Halting a good fifty yards from the stream, Rye sat quietly in the shade of a broadly spreading cottonwood, listening for sounds that would indicate the presence of others. Hearing nothing and noting no odor of tobacco or anything else out of the ordinary on the slight breeze, he moved on.

Reaching the creek, the marshal dismounted and let the chestnut slake its thirst while he took down his canteen and refilled it. Noman's-land would be new country to him, and when he would again cross a stream in the days to come he could only guess. That chore out of the way, he set the container aside, brushed back his hat, and washed his face and neck, removing the crust of blood, sweat, and dust. But he conceded no more to personal comfort; he had already lost too much time.

Rising, he hung the canteen on the horn, and moving away from the chestnut, began to explore the soft mud along the bank of the creek. He found no sign of hoofprints in the first reasonable stretch of ground, and returning to the gelding, he mounted. Slack on the saddle, Rye considered the country behind him thoughtfully.

The box canyon where the hideout stood was somewhat to the south, he judged. The outlaws could be expected to have taken a direct route for the territory border. He was probably a bit too far north. Coming to that conclusion, the lawman swung about and headed downstream.

A quarter hour later, with dark clouds now beginning to mask the sky, he pulled up short. Before him was a welter of hoofprints in the dark, soft soil. The outlaws had ridden into the water, probably halted long enough for their horses to drink, and moved on. He would be better able to make a count on the opposite bank as the outlaws, entering the creek in a group, would likely pull out one or two at a time, all depending on the varying thirsts of the animals.

There were seven in the party. Rye, hunched at the edge of the stream's east side moments later, found it easy to make the determination; but whether Harry Wilse was one of the number he had no way of telling.

Mulling it over in his mind, figuring the time elapsed between the escape of the main party of outlaws and that of Wilse, it would seem that Harry would be only a few minutes behind. Going back onto the saddle, Rye continued on downstream at a slow walk. Almost at once he came onto a single set of prints entering the creek from the west and emerging on the opposite side.

They had to be made by Wilse's horse, but the lawman could only guess how old the tracks were—not that it mattered particularly. The point was that Harry Wilse was hurrying to join the other members of his gang, and all would then follow the usual procedure of holing up at some specific place in No-man's-land. Rye had considered the possibility that, badly disorganized after the shootout at the hideout, the outlaws might scatter. But there was proof now that the established routine was not being broken.

Satisfied, Rye went back onto the saddle and rode away from the creek in a due-east direction. The border could not be more than another hour or so away, and he wanted to be well within the lawless strip by dark. Once there, and with sunlight gone, he'd have a good chance of spotting the outlaws' campfire.

Rye had no way of knowing when he crossed over, simply judging that it had been accomplished when darkness, under a now completely gray sky, closed in. He pressed on without halting, however, riding the rim of a deep arroyo that carved its irregular slash through a broad land of buttes, washes, and rolling hills as it snaked eastward, knowing only that it was taking him deeper into the country where no law was recognized.

That latter fact did not trouble John Rye, and that he might in actuality be breaking the law in extending his authority into an area where the government for which he worked had no jurisdiction received even less consideration. He was charged with the capture, or elimination, of certain outlaws known to be guilty of crimes—and to the fulfillment of that end he would proceed, regardless.

Twice, late that afternoon, Rye saw what he took to be dust in the distance, but he could not be sure, and finally, after night had set in solidly and he deemed further travel pointless, he pulled the tired chestnut to a halt.

The best course to follow now was make a light camp—and wait, hoping a campfire somewhere about him in the distance would designate the outlaws' location. They would not bother to take precautions; such were needless since they were well within No-man's-land and enjoying the protection it provided.

It was possible they would make no night camp, but would instead continue on until they reached an established hideout such as they made use of in the box canyon on the side of Big Mountain.

He recalled then words spoken by T.J. Yocum—or was it Frank Pace?—to the effect that the outlaws could be holing up in an abandoned ranchhouse when the law pressed them. That would explain why Rye could see no signs of them and their campfire. Rye sighed heavily as he accepted that strong possibility; it meant that from then on it would be a matter of tracking—and that was not going to be easy.

Pulled in beside a cluster of cedars, Rye dug into his saddlebags for his grub sack, selected a portion of dried beef and a few biscuits, and dropped to his haunches. He elected to pass up making coffee; a fire might be seen by the outlaws and set them to wondering.

The meal finished, washed down by a swallow of water from his canteen, Rye unrolled his blanket and stretched out in the cool blackness to get a few hours' rest. But he placed himself so as to face the east; he had not entirely forsaken the thought that Wilse and his men would make a night camp, and their campfire—

The marshal came to sudden alert. Somewhere back along the rim of the arroyo along which he had followed, he caught the sound of an approaching horse. He was being trailed.

CHAPTER XVII

Rising swiftly, Rye drifted quietly away from the scrub trees. Hand resting on the butt of his pistol, he drew off into the shadows of a second group of cedars. There, eyes straining to penetrate the darkness, he waited.

Moments later he saw a solitary rider, a vague shape hunched on the saddle—he could determine little else. It might be one of the outlaws, delayed in his escape for some reason—possibly even Harry Wilse, as there was no real proof that he had rejoined his friends. The marshal's jaw hardened in satisfaction. If true, he not only would have Wilse but know also that he was on the right trail to find the others.

The rider drew nearer, his horse walking slowly, head bobbing up and down, hoofs muted by the soft sand. Rye wished there'd been time to move the chestnut so there would be no sign of his presence and thus make it even easier, but it hadn't been possible—and it didn't matter. Abruptly the dark shapes were abreast the gelding. The rider straightened, pulling his mount to a sudden stop.

"Rye—"

Anger whipped through the marshal. It was Frank Pace. Stepping out of the shadows, he faced the lawman.

"What the hell are you doing here?" he demanded.

Pace swung off his horse slowly. "Keep your shirt on," he said quietly, looping the reins of his buckskin about a limb of a cedar. His tone was cool, reflecting the resentment he'd earlier displayed. "Figured you'd be farther along than this," he added, coming about.

"That concerns me, not you," Rye said coldly. "Answer my question."

Pace shrugged. "I was sent to do a job, same as you and the others—"

"Under my orders," the marshal cut in, "but you've got ideas of your own—and I won't go for that."

"Which is the same as saying you're always right, and nobody else ever is."

John Rye let that hang for a long breath. "I'm not about to start arguing all over again with you, Frank—I've got neither the time nor the patience, but I'll listen to any man who knows what he's talking about and comes up with something better than I've got in mind."

"That ain't how it seems to me. Far as I can tell, you got such a big opinion of yourself—all that doomsday marshal bull and the like—that you don't ever figure you're wrong about anything."

"I've been wrong plenty of times," Rye said evenly, holding onto his temper, "but that's not what this's all about. You were to work under me—my orders. Instead you decided to go off on your own back there at the house, messed up what was a sure-fire deal that would've gotten us Wilse and his whole bunch. Now you're out of line again. If you wanted to do something, why didn't you give Gannon a hand? He's got four prisoners and two wounded men besides a bunch of women and a couple of hired hands to look out for; instead you turn your back on him and show up here. I want to know why."

"On account of this," Pace said slowly, distinctly. "I figure I'm just as good a lawman as you, and I've got as much right as you to be in on laying Harry Wilse by the heels."

"Maybe. Thinking back over the way you handled things, I've got my doubts."

"I don't give a hoot in hell about your doubtings. It could just as well been me they picked to run this posse, only I ain't had your luck in making the right friends setting up in high places."

Rye swore impatiently. "Pace, you sound like some kid arguing over nothing! Now, I want you to mount up and get out of here. If you want to work, go give Hugh Gannon a hand; otherwise head on back to where you're from."

"I ain't about to do neither," Pace said stubbornly. "I belong here."

"Not with me. I'll tell you straight out—I don't trust you."

Pace stirred angrily. "That's a hell of a thing to say to a man! Plain truth is you need me— bad, only you won't own up to it."

"I could use some help, all right—but somebody I can rely on. You don't fill the bill."

"That's what you think! What do you know about me, anyway, other'n I didn't do exactly like you told me?"

"That's enough for me," Rye said cooly.

"No it ain't! I've handled just as many hardcase killers as you."

"Could be you have. I'm not one to keep books on something like that."

"And I've been wearing a badge long as you have, maybe even longer."

"Plenty other men can say that," the marshal replied indifferently. "What're you getting at?"

"That you ain't one whit better'n me when it comes to being a lawman, and you've got no call to badmouth me just because you don't like the way I do things."

Rye shrugged, turning away from Pace. The senseless wrangling was wearing on Rye's nerves—and he had work to do. Shifting his eyes to the dark land stretching out toward the east, he swept it with a searching glance; no sign of a campfire.

"You want to know why you're needing me bad?" Pace continued, moving around to where he faced Rye.

"I can't think of a reason—"

"Well, you do, and I'll tell you why if you ain't too bullheaded to admit it when I'm done. You're riding blind, looking for Wilse and his bunch. I can take you where they'll be, ninety-nine chances out of a hundred."

Rye gave that thought. It had been Pace and not T.J. Yocum who had mentioned an old ranchhouse where the outlaws would ride to.

"You got any idea where it is?" Pace persisted.

"No," Rye answered truthfully. "Ahead, I know that. I'll find it."

"Maybe in a couple of days. I can have you there by sunup."

Rye settled his full attention on the man. In the weak light, Pace's features were barely visible.

"This some kind of a trick—or the truth?"

"The gospel truth! I'm offering to take you to where Wilse'n them'll be holed up, and be in on the kill with you. You'll be needing me for that, unless you're plumb loco. Going to be eight or ten of them, and you ain't got the chance of a grasshopper in a chicken yard of coming out alive when the shooting starts if you try it alone."

Rye hesitated, giving the lawman's words consideration. There was no doubt he spoke the truth insofar as time saved in searching out the outlaws was concerned. And he was not fool enough to believe he could take on near a dozen gunmen and escape with his life. Of course, bracing them all at the same moment wouldn't be in his plan; in fact, he'd not figured that far ahead as yet, being a believer in first things first. Once he had located the outlaws, then the necessity for a plan would be at hand.

But could he trust Frank Pace?

The lawman had revealed his feeling for him, one of hatred or at least bordering on it, several times. In a showdown could he depend on Pace to stand by him, or was Pace likely to hold back, let the outlaws have a free hand—or possibly turn his own gun on him? Bitterness ran deep enough in Pace to cause him to do so.

But there would be tremendous advantage in getting to the outlaws by morning, and that outweighed the possibility of Pace seizing a moment to satisfy a personal grudge. Rye would chance it, take care to keep a wary eye on the lawman, and try not to present him with any tempting opportunities. One thing for certain: He'd place no reliance in him.

"All right, Pace, we'll do this together. I'd as soon not waste a lot of time tracking—"

"Now you're being real smart," Pace said, his voice filled with satisfaction. "When do you want to move out?"

"Now. You said we could be there by daylight. Let's do it."

CHAPTER XVIII

The night continued dark as no stars shone through the overcast and the moon remained nonexistent. The coyotes and wolves were silent, and the only indications of life around them as they rode steadily on was the hooting of an owl off in the arroyo along which they traveled.

"You recollect a fellow called Jamison, Marshal?"

Rye repeated the name, rolled it about in his memory, and found it unfamiliar. "Sure don't."

"You ought," Pace said. "Was about two years ago. Held up a stage over Nebraska way. Killed the driver, the shotgun rider, and one of the passengers."

Rye shrugged and stared off into the soft blackness that covered the land. "Some special reason I should know him?"

"Reckon there is. You ran him down."

Something began to stir in the lawman's mind, but he could not bring it to the surface.

"Like I said, I don't keep track of the outlaws I bring in."

"You didn't bring him in—you shot him dead, not that he didn't have it coming, but you sure cheated me out of a fat reward."

"You after him, too?"

"Yeh. Was sheriffing over there at the time. All happened in my county, and he was mine to collect on. You horned in, cut me out of it."

The tautness in Frank Pace's voice bespoke a barely restrained anger, and conveyed to Rye also a clue as to why Pace was so antagonistic.

"Can't say I horned in," Rye said evenly. "Jobs I do are ones I'm sent on—I don't pick them. . . . We anywhere close to the hideout?" he added, glancing to the east. A faint glare was beginning to show in the dark sky.

"Ain't far now. . . . Another time, too, you cost me—"

"I don't want to hear about it," the marshal cut in wearily.

"You're going to, anyway. Outlaw by the name of Harley Moss—"

Rye, taxed finally to his utter limit, pulled his horse to an abrupt stop. He swung sharply about and faced Frank Pace.

"Forget it!" he snarled. "I'm calling a halt to this right here. Turn around and head back. Frank. I've had all of you I want."

Pace, shoulders slumped, both hands resting on the horn of his saddle, stirred, spitting into the weeds. "I just want you to know a couple of things—"

"I can live without it!"

"Sure, maybe so, but I figured you ought to know why—"

"I don't want to hear anything from you! I'm here to do a job—one you're insisting on taking a hand in. I can damn well do it without you—or with you. Won't matter to me which, but you've come this far and—"

"Only making conversation," Pace protested lamely.

"I'll get by without that, too. I'm not going to say this again, Frank: Keep your mouth shut, or pull out."

Pace was silent for a time, head cocked, face tipped down as he studied Rye through narrowed eyes. A hard smile cracked his tightly set lips. "Whatever you say, Marshal," he murmured.

They rode on, keeping to the edge of the big wash, and then shortly, as the first flare of color began to fill the east above the horizon, they came to a sharp bend in the arroyo.

"There it is," Pace said, pointing off to his left.

John Rye had already seen the house—a squat, adobe affair in the shadow of a fairly high bluff. Smoke was rising from a stovepipe chimney, and lamplight glowed in the windows. Several horses were standing, hip-shot, along a hitchrack, but it was impossible to make an exact count.

Evidently long unused for anything other than a hideout, brush and weeds had crept in from the surrounding areas, covering the yard and giving the place a wild, neglected appearance.

"You been inside?" Rye asked, beckoning to Pace as they cut back along the arroyo and rode down into it.

"Nope, just sort of went by a time ago."

Gaining the sandy floor of the wash along which a tiny stream of water wound its way, they doubled back toward the structure, keeping well in the high growth of rabbitbush, plume, doveweed, and the like growing along its banks.

"There another door around back?" Rye asked.

"Yep. You can look right down on it from that little hill behind the place."

Rye lifted his glance to the mound of weeds, rocks, and reddish soil east of the shack. He shook his head.

"Too far. Got to be where we can move in fast. Let's get a bit closer."

Rye could see the horses better now—eight of them lined up at the rack. Wilse had joined the others, as could be expected. Thoughtful, the marshal continued along the arroyo, pointing for a deep cutback where another wash, angling down from the higher plains, formed an intersection.

They had just reached it when the front door of the house opened and two men came out. Neither was familiar to Rye, or to Pace. The two men from the house paused in the overgrown yard, yawned, stretched, and then moved toward the horses.

"They're leaving," Pace muttered and drew his pistol.

"No," Rye said, quickly staying the lawman's hand by gripping his arm.

"Hell with that!" Frank Pace snapped, jerking away. "We're here to put an end to that bunch of bastards. Might as well begin now."

"I said to forget it," Rye repeated. "They're a couple of small fry, and we're after the big ones—Harry Wilse, Calloway, Berino, and the like. Cutting down on that pair'll tip off the others that we're out here."

Pace settled back, grumbling to himself. "All right, have it your way," he said. "I sure hate letting any of them get away."

"Same here, but I'll give up a couple of penny-ante saloon bums anytime if it'll help me get my hands on Wilse and his kind."

"Yeh, guess so—"

The two outlaws had mounted and were swinging out of the yard and heading up a trail that led northward out of the arroyo.

"Going to Kansas," Pace said, again at low breath. "Be the last we'll see of them."

Rye paid no heed to Pace; Rye's attention was centered on the house and its adjacent area. They would have little difficulty in approaching it on foot; brush screened the structure, and there, was only a narrow band of open ground running along its walls. They would need to either draw the outlaws into the open, or gain the inside themselves, he concluded, as the thick adobe walls, impenetrable by bullets even at close range, made a fortress of the place.

"How you aiming to take them?" Pace asked. He was still fuming over allowing the two lesser members of the gang to ride off unchallenged.

"We can't just wait around hoping they'll come out," Rye said, again studying the solidly built structure. Lamplight no longer showed in the small windows, set singly and high in each wall. "We go in after them—one of us taking the front door, the other the back."

Frank Pace smiled, and nodded his approval. "Just what I'd say to do. We bust in on them, open up with our .45s before they know what's going on."

"Which door do you want?"

"I'll take the back."

"Suits me," Rye said. "I'll move up through the brush, find me a spot close. You work your way around to the back, get yourself set. How much time do you want? We need to hit both doors at pretty much the same moment."

Pace gave the distance from the cutback to the rear of the house a calculating glance. "Fifteen minutes."

Rye drew out his watch and consulted its Roman numerals. Frank Pace, following suit, examined his timepiece.

"Fifteen minutes be enough?" the marshal asked.

"Going to be a-plenty—"

"All right. We'll move in at three minutes to five—let's make it exactly five o'clock."

"I'll be ready; just you be goddamn sure you are," Pace said, returning his watch to its pocket and, bending low, began to make his way through the dense growth for the rear of the shack.

CHAPTER XIX

As Rye watched Frank Pace slip off into the brush, the thought came to him that he may have again made a mistake in placing any sort of trust and dependence on the man. It might have been wiser had he stood firm back at the cedars when Pace appeared out of the dark, and insisted that he turn back, help Hugh Gannon, or pull out altogether.

Such could have led to a serious problem, however. Pace had assumed a stubborn attitude, adamant in his desire to take part in bringing in Harry Wilse and his outlaw followers. It could have come down to driving the man off at gunpoint, and that wasn't practical—or sensible. Regardless, it was too late to think about it now. Rye could only hope that Pace wouldn't, in some way, foul up this plan.

Checking his pistols, the marshal dropped to a crouch and forged a path through the tangled, dense growth until he was directly opposite the entrance to the old adobe. He was no more than ten yards away from the iron-strapped slab panel at that point, near enough in fact to hear faintly the low mutter of voices.

Squatted on his heels, Rye looked at his watch. Ten minutes until the stipulated time. Restoring the piece, the marshal considered what he must do. At exactly five o'clock he would come to his feet, run across the intervening ground, and with a gun in each hand, burst through the doorway, hopefully ajar or not too sturdily affixed.

If everything went according to plan, Frank Pace would be doing the same from the rear. The element of surprise would be with them, and they should take the outlaws off guard, and finding themselves between Pace and him, each holding two pistols, Wilse and his friends—five in number, if you went by the count of the horses—would likely offer no resistance.

A disturbing thought crept into John Rye's mind. He would be on the opposite side of the room, perhaps directly so, from Pace when each came into the old adobe. It would be easy for a stray bullet from Frank Pace's gun to find its mark in him if the man's ill feeling ran that deep. Jubilee Jensen had suspected it did—and Rye had had his own wonder, but there was nothing he could do now. He'd have to gamble on it, at least during those first few moments, hope that—

The sudden crackle of gunshots filled the arroyo, setting up a chain of echoes rolling across the slopes and down the wash. Rye jerked upright, an oath on his lips. The shooting had come from the rear of the house. Either Pace had moved in too soon, or had carelessly allowed himself to be seen.

John Rye wasted no time on speculation. If he was to bring down Harry Wilse and his gang, he would need to act now, immediately, before the outlaws scattered.

Sucking in a deep breath, pistol in each hand, the lawman lunged out of the brush across the narrow strip of open ground. He reached the door, hesitated, raised a foot, and drove it against the panel. It swung inward with a crash, and he rushed in.

Wilse and his friends were gathered about the open doorway at the other side of the room. Beyond them in the yard Rye could see Frank Pace sprawled half in, half out of the brush.

As the outlaws spun in surprise to face Rye, Wilse reacted instantly. He ducked low, throwing himself through the doorway. Calloway and the others started to follow. The *vaquero*, caught against the jamb, was unable to move. Gun already in his hand—evidently he was the one who had spotted Pace and brought him down—he whirled.

Rye gave the Mexican no opportunity to use his weapon. Rye fired point blank with both pistols. The bullets drove into the *vaquero's* chest, slamming him against the wall. As the Mexican began to sink to the dusty floor, Rye triggered his guns a second time and dropped Max Omer on the stoop just outside.

A third man—short, redheaded, and a stranger to the marshal—appeared suddenly in the doorway, the gun in his hand bucking. Rye felt the touch of bullets fired too hurriedly, and heard them thud into the solid mud bricks behind him.

Cool, coiling, acrid powder smoke hanging about him, Rye stepped to one side. The red-head, giving way, was briefly squared in the rectangle of the entrance. The law man shot him down and moved on. Wilse, Calloway, Kincaid—they were the important ones, the men he wanted most of all. Time after time they had managed to give the law the slip, and then reappear to ply their outlaw trade; at all cost he had to put an end to that.

Rye gained the door. The three men would be outside, weapons trained on the opening as they waited for him to step into view. Grim, the marshal holstered one of his pistols. Reaching down, he grasped the body of Max Omer by the collar and dragged it upright. Holding it in front of him, he pushed the dead outlaw ahead of him into the open.

Instantly there was a hammer of shooting. Rye saw Calloway and Kincaid at the corner of the house. Wilse was a step or two back of them. As Omer's body jolted from the bullets fired, Rye sent a leaden slug into Calloway. The outlaw went down, flinging both arms wide. Immediately Harry Wilse and Kincaid dodged around the corner of the house, apparently making for the brush on the north side of the yard.

Releasing his grip on Omer's body and letting it fall, Rye reloaded quickly, hurriedly crossed the back of the house, and halted at the corner. He could only guess where the two men were—somewhere in the dense undergrowth, he was sure. He'd have to circle wide and try to come in on them from behind.

The dry scrape of a boot heel on wood brought John Rye up short. A voice—taunting, snide, filled with satisfaction—reached him.

"Don't move, Marshal—and drop that iron you're holding."

Rye hesitated briefly, and then taut, released his grip on his pistol, allowing it to fall. He'd figured wrong. He'd made a bad mistake—and it was going to cost him his life. He swore silently.

"Turn around—real slow."

The marshal came about. It wasn't Wilse, he knew; therefore it had to be Jack Kincaid. It was. The squat, bearded outlaw, dark eyes glittering, grinned at him.

"I want you to see this bullet coming," he said through clenched teeth.

Rye, cool as always at such moments, shook his head. "Put it down, Jack. You're under arrest."

Kincaid's eyes flared in surprise. "By God!" he exclaimed. "You're sure the one! You got the guts of an Army mule."

"I'm the law," Rye said quietly. "I know right where I stand. You're going to hang, and if I don't take you in for it there'll be another marshal come along who will."

Kincaid laughed. "You all ain't done much good so far," he drawled.

There was movement beyond the outlaw and to his right. Pace—the man was still alive, had raised his head slightly, and was listening and watching. This should please him—seeing Rye shot down.

"You're wrong there, Jack," Rye said.

"There's only you and Harry left. The rest are all dead or headed for jail and the rope."

"Maybe, but Harry and me's all that counts. We can scrape up a-plenty wanting to throw in with us."

"Not after today. You've lost it all."

Jack Kincaid seemed to consider that, his brow pulling into a tight frown. The sun had now reached above the hills to the east, and down the arroyo a jay was scolding noisily. The outlaw spat abruptly.

"You're plain full of bull," he snarled and raised his pistol higher. "This here's sure going to give me a good feeling, blasting you. Say howdy to that other badge toter Berino caught sneaking up on us when you get to hell."

He'd not go down without making a try at stopping Kincaid, Rye resolved. He still had his spare gun in the holster. Turned partly, the outlaw had not noticed it, satisfied when Rye dropped his other weapon. There might be a chance he could draw and put a bullet into Kincaid before life ended.

"So long, Marshal," the outlaw said derisively. "Now, you be sure and give my howdies to—"

The crash of a gunshot cut off Kincaid's words. The outlaw jolted, staggering into the wall of the house, the weapon in his hand tipping down as strength abruptly failed him.

Rye threw a glance at Frank Pace. The lawman had raised himself onto his elbows and was holding his .45 by both hands. A wry, painful grin curved his lips.

"Chalk—that'n up—to me," he said with effort.

John Rye nodded. Pace had saved his life. The man he believed would as soon put a bullet into him himself to satisfy what he considered past wrongs had used his ebbing strength to pull the trigger of his gun and stop Jack Kincaid. How could he have midjudged the man so badly? Or was Rye right, and at the last, critical moment the lawman in Pace had come to the fore? That seemed more likely, but no matter now. He should go to Frank, see if there was anything he could do for him, but Harry Wilse was still somewhere around, hoping no doubt to get in a shot.

"Hang on," Rye called. "Quick as I root Harry out I'll be back."

"He ducked—into that brush—there—other side of—that big rock," Pace said in a dragging voice, and then added: "Ain't—no big—hurry. I—I sure ain't—going—nowheres."

CHAPTER XX

Rye, keeping low, darted across the open ground, gaining the tall rabbitbush and oak that fringed the yard. The rock Frank Pace had spoken of was a short distance ahead and to his left. Beyond it, thanks to a consatnt supply of water from the small stream coursing down the arroyo, the brush grew tangled and dense with an occasional cedar tree or boulder showing through.

Wilse was either holding back, expecting Jack Kincaid to handle the chore of disposing of their enemies, or else endeavoring to get himself placed where he would be afforded an open shot somewhere in that wild area. Halting, Rye gave it quick thought. He'd be a fool to rush head-on, blindly, into the heavy undergrowth.

Pivoting, he cut back through the thick shrubbery and moved parallel to the rock that Pace had indicated. It would be better to get away from the house, circle wide, and try to come in on the outlaw from the rear. With a bit of care and a little luck, Rye should be able to pull it off without Wilse seeing him.

A good fifty yards covered, Rye began to double back, moving slowly, quietly, careful to dislodge no loose gravel or allow the springy growth to scrape against him and set up a distinctive sound. Shortly he caught sight of the rock. Wilse was not to be seen. Frowning, the lawman raised himself higher for a better look. He had been certain the outlaw—

The dry rattle of rocks somewhere beyond the boulder came to him. Wilse had seen him and was moving off. At once Rye hurried on, hoping for a glimpse of the man. After a few moments Rye paused. There was no sign of Harry Wilse and no further sounds of his activity.

Rigid, the marshal waited, ears and eyes straining to determine the whereabouts of the outlaw. Sweat lay on Rye's forehead in a warm, moist blanket, and reaching up, he wiped it away with the back of a hand. Off somewhere in the brush, a prairie dog barked a shrill warning of danger, and high overhead in the cloud-spotted sky, vultures were beginning to gather, drawn by that mysterious instinct that motivates them when death is present.

A gun racketed through the quiet. Reflex action dropped Rye to his haunches. Again he frowned, puzzled. No bullet had passed by. There had been no clipping of leaves in the bushes, no spurt of dust, no whining sound as the slug, striking rock, caromed off into space.

But there had been a gunshot, and fired by a man like Wilse, it could hardly have gone so wide. Crouched, Rye endeavored to fix the source of the sound in his mind. It seemed to him that it had come from the other end of the wash, somewhat below the point where he and Frank Pace had begun their approach to the house.

Still low, Rye moved forward in the direction he judged Wilse would be. Rye was angling through the thickest stand of the brush and after a dozen yards he halted, breathing hard from his efforts. The muscles of his back and legs were protesting the hunched position he was being compelled to maintain.

A displaced rock rolled down a short slope, bounding and rattling briefly. It was to his right. Instantly the lawman wheeled to face that new direction. Coming almost fully upright, he searched the shadowy brush for the outlaw.

An impatient oath ripped from Rye's lips. It was an aggravating, frustrating game of deadly hide-and-seek, and it was beginning to wear him down. Why the hell didn't Harry make a stand behind a rock or a tree and shoot it out with him? The advantage would certainly be with the outlaw. Could it be that Harry Wilse, realizing he was completely alone, that his followers—the men he depended on—were all dead, had lost his nerve?

It was beginning to look that way, Rye decided, moving on toward the point where the rock had fallen. He could last as long as Harry at the game—and sooner or later he would get his look at the outlaw. That would be all he'd need—one glimpse. Wilse would never shake him after that.

Reaching the edge of the arroyo, Rye paused. The rock had apparently been displaced from the top of the short embankment, from where it had tumbled to the graveled floor below. How could Wilse have been there, several feet above the arroyo bed, and gone unseen?

Rye turned and glanced to the east. The upper third of the old adobe house was visible. He had gone a considerable distance from it in his pursuit of the outlaw. Clearly, Wilse was running blindly, desperately, doing his utmost to keep out of sight. Hunched low, the lawman crossed to a break in the wall of brush, clawing his way to its rim. There he threw his glance about. The growth was sparser to his right, and more cedars were to be seen; but there was no indication of Harry Wilse.

Over to his left in a confusion of rocks and clumps of Apache plume, Rye heard a thump followed by the rattle of gravel. He shifted his attention to that position instantly—a good fifty yards distant—and had a quick glimpse of a fist-size stone rolling down a short slope.

Rye swore again as understanding came to him. He had been tricked. Wilse was pulling him away from the house, traveling in a wide circle while suckering him on with sounds created by tossing rocks off into the brush. It could mean only one thing: Harry Wilse, wanting to avoid a showdown, as the lawman suspected, was trying to reach the horses standing at the hitchrack. He was trying to lead Rye as far from the yard as possible.

The marshal grinned tightly. Two could play the game as well as one. Stepping into the open,

Rye exposed himself briefly and made as if to move forward toward the decoying sound. And then ducking low, he dropped to the floor of the arroyo. Wheeling, and well in the thick brush, he cut back on a direct line for the house, moving fast, halting finally when he came to the narrow strip of cleared ground that surrounded the structure.

Breathing heavily, hunkered in the tangled growth, he considered the probable location of the outlaw at that moment. He would be somewhere on the opposite side of the shack, working toward the horses, confident the man searching for him was at the upper end of the wash checking out the noise made by a tossed stone.

Only this time it wasn't going to work. Harry had overplayed his hand. Rye, keeping the building between him and the hitchrack, hurriedly crossed the yard, stepped over the bodies sprawled in the doorway of the house, and entered.

He cast a glance at Frank Pace as he stepped inside. The lawman, watching him silently, stirred, signifying that he was still alive.

Rye nodded, and careful to make no sound, quickly gained the opposite side of the room and drew up at the front entrance. The horses, heads low as they dozed wearily in the mounting heat, were to his left. Tense, the marshal waited. He hadn't been wrong in assuming Wilse was endeavoring to trick him, he was certain, but the outlaw should be making his move, unless—

John Rye's thoughts came to a stop. Harry

Wilse was suddenly standing at the edge of the brush beyond the horses. Crouched, face gleaming with sweat, he glanced about, and deciding after a few moments that he was in the clear, started across the yard for the hitchrack. Rye delayed until the outlaw was well away from the brush, and then stepped into the open.

"Wilse—"

The outlaw jolted as if struck. He came to a halt, eyes spreading with surprise.

"Get your hands up, Harry—"

Wilse eased back, eyes now narrowing. A hard grin split his lips. "I figured you was up at the other end of the wash."

"I got wise to you," Rye said dryly.

"Had you going there for a bit—"

"Yeah, reckon you did. Get your hands up, Harry. I don't want to kill you."

"The hell with you, Rye!" Wilse shouted. He made a stab for the gun on his hip. "I ain't hanging—"

Rye drew fast and clean. His bullet smashed into Harry Wilse before the outlaw's pistol had cleared leather, knocking him back and down as the horses, startled by the gun's blast, began to jerk and tug at the lines tying them to the hitchrack in a futile attempt to break free.

For a long minute the marshal stood motionless in the streaming sunlight as dust from the churning hoofs of the horses, mixing with powder smoke, spun about him, and then his head came up and his shoulders squared themselves into their usual rigid line.

Raising his pistol, he flipped open the loading gate, punched out the spent cartridge, thumbed a fresh load into the cylinder, and holstered the weapon. Without a further glance at Harry Wilse—a completed chore now relegated to the past—he hurried to where Frank Pace lay.

CHAPTER XXI

Pace had not moved, and still lay face down at the edge of the yard. Rye knelt beside him.

"Frank—"

The lawman turned his head. His eyes were dull, and there was a sallowness to his windburned skin. "Yeh?"

"You hit bad?"

"Plenty. Right—through the—belly," Pace said with effort. "Ain't no sense—talking about packing—me in to—some doc. Never make it. Just—don't move me—none. I'm—all right—laying here."

"Whatever you say."

"You—get Harry?"

"Yeh. Tried tricking me off into the brush so's he could get to his horse. Didn't work out."

"He—he always was a—slick one," Pace muttered, and forced a grin. "Reckon you're—satisfied now. You got them—all."

Rye shrugged. "It's what I was sent to do,

151

along with you and the others. The order was to put an end to Wilse and his gang. We did."

A shudder swept through Frank Pace. He swallowed hard and seemed to take a grip on himself. "I was a plain fool—pulling the—stunt I did."

Rye made no comment. The hard, humorless grin once more pulled at Pace's mouth. "Not asking—your pardon. Never—get it. Ain't in a—hard-nosed sonofabitch—like you—to forgive a man—nothing when it comes—comes to crossing—up you—and the law. Reckon I—wasn't thinking straight. Only—excuse I—got. You—can take it—or go to hell."

Rye smiled. "You're wasting your breath. Anyway, I owe you, Frank. Hadn't been for you putting that bullet in Jack Kincaid, I'd be dead right now."

Pace's lips curled. "With—with your kind—of luck? I ain't taking—no odds on it. He'd probably missed and—you'd plugged—him."

"Doubt that," the marshal said. "Anything I can do for you when it's over?"

"Nope—sure ain't. No family—so there's nobody—caring what—happens—to—me. As soon—you'd plant me—right around here—close. Be—a waste of time—toting me in—to some—damned—graveyard. Over—there in the shade—of them—cedars. A good—place."

Another tremor wracked Pace. He rolled slightly to one side and slid a hand slowly, tentatively across the sandy ground toward Rye. The marshal reached down, enclosed it in his own, and pressed it firmly.

"Give—give 'em hell—John," Pace murmured and went completely slack.

Rye drew himself upright, eyes on the dead lawman. Jubilee Jensen . . . Bob Shuster . . . Frank Pace—all dead. Joe Dix . . . T.J. Yocum—shot up, just how badly Rye didn't really know. The posse sent to wipe out the Wilse gang had paid a hell of a price, but he supposed it was worth it; they had succeeded.

He walked across the yard to the house, and entering, hunted about until he found a rusty spade among the tools left there by the previous owner. Returning to the yard, he selected a place at the edge of the wash, beyond the reach of high water, and dug a large grave. In it he laid the bodies of Harry Wilse and his outlaw followers, wrapped in their blankets, and with their guns, and covered them over not only with the loose soil but also with as many rocks as he could find close by.

That done, Rye went to the cluster of cedars Frank Pace had indicated and hollowed out a second grave. Here the ground was much harder and was laced with tough roots and studded with stones, but he managed a fairly deep excavation.

Soaked with sweat by the time the job was finished, shoulders aching from such unaccustomed labors, he wrapped the lawman in his blanket also and buried him there in the shade as he'd requested. He left both graves unmarked, believing it not only wiser, but that there was little point.

The circling vultures that had gathered overhead were still present—great, broad-winged, silent shadows maintaining a sharp-eyed vigil—and casting a glance at them, he turned his attention to the horses after first bringing up his own chestnut and Pace's buckskin and tying them at the hitchrack.

Removing the gear from all but his gelding, Rye piled it inside the house. The outlaws' horses, and Frank Pace's buckskin, free of restricting leather, immediately began to drift off, moving down the arroyo. Rye could see a cluster of cottonwoods in the near distance and reckoned there would be a stand of grass there. With ample water and forage available, the animals would do all right until claimed by someone.

All chores deemed necessary completed, the marshal mounted, rode back up onto the flat above the wash, and turned toward Big Mountain. He was not entirely finished with the job as yet; he must know for certain that his order to burn down the outlaw hideout in the canyon had been fulfilled. Only then would he be able to make an honest and satisfactory report to headquarters.

The hours were beginning to tell on Rye, and as the chestnut moved steadily on, alternatively walking and loping as suited the contours of the land, the lawman dozed. Never one to need any great amount of sleep, he found it easy to catch up on lost minutes while traveling.

Hunger, too, finally made itself felt, and when he reached the creek around midafternoon where he had, that previous day, gotten a line on the outlaws, he pulled up.

Leaving the saddle, he built a fire and brought out his grubsack. He was down to basics—a bit of coffee, some dried beef, a few biscuits, and, happily, a tin of peaches. He made a meal of this, resting in the coolness along the stream for an hour while he did, and then going back onto the gelding, continued on his way.

Gannon, with the wounded Joe Dix and T.J. Yocum shepherding their prisoners and the hangers-on, would be in Trinidad by then, he presumed. It wasn't a trip involving too many miles, and unless they had experienced trouble of some sort, they would have easily made it in a day.

He wondered about Dix, recalling his last minutes with the Arizona lawman. Did Dix still feel as he had about Ruby's death—placing the blame for it on Rye instead of Harry Wilse, who had been the one to fire the fatal bullet?

Rye supposed that, from the angle Joe had witnessed the incident, it could have looked as if he were the one, but in actuality, he had been well to the side, taking care to not trap Ruby and the other women in the crossfire. Likely Dix had realized that by now.

The combination of pain and grief had twisted Dix's mind to the point where he believed what he thought he saw while totally ignoring the facts. It was a sad thing for Joe, and his angry denunciation should be overlooked. No doubt he was regretting the harsh accusation that undoubtedly was weighing heavily on his conscience by that time.

Rye raised his eyes and studied the distance. Big Mountain was looming ahead. The sky had cleared late that morning and was now a clear, washed blue, although there had been no welcome rain. The heat was making itself felt but had not reached the point where it was uncomfortable.

Noisy jays flitted about in the trees, scolding

him for his passage, and once he startled a mule deer doe, sending her bounding off, stiff-legged, through the trees. Hardened man though he was to the all too often brutal facts of life, Rye rode with a heavy heart. Shuster . . . Jubilee Jensen . . . Frank Pace, despite his drawbacks, were good men, and the country, beset by outlawry, could ill lose them. And the list could be longer: T.J. and Dix may have been added to it.

Was Rye at fault? He had been the one to plan the raid on the outlaw hideout, had assigned each of the lawmen to a particular job. Could he have planned better? Was he to blame for the loss of the men? Had he taken on too big a job with too few, as Pace had claimed, and needlessly sacrified the men supporting him?

John Rye squarely faced the disturbing questions put to him by his conscience. He had done what he thought best, and in his judgment, necessary. His scheme had been carefully thought out. It had seemed to him to be practical and one that would be to the best advantage of the lawmen backing him—yet it had gone wrong; and while the end result was all that could be asked for insofar as the outlaws were concerned, it was difficult to accept the cost.

He hoped he'd not again be called upon to recruit the aid of other lawmen. He much preferred to work alone, thus not only confining responsibility but also the possibility of death to himself.

Rye slowed the chestnut. The box canyon where Harry Wilse and his friends had established their headquarters was just ahead. He sniffed at the quiet air, catching the rank smell of burned wood. Hugh Gannon had done the job, he reckoned, but he rode on. It was still necessary that he have a firsthand look.

Turning up the slope, he reached the clearing where the lawmen had been waiting for him, with the bodies of Bob Shuster and Jubilee Jensen, and their prisoners. He continued, coming finally to the open ground where the house, with its sheds and corrals, had stood.

All were now charred, blackened ruins. Smoke was twisting upward in small, thin coils from several points, and the rock chimneys, like stone fingers rising out of the desolate ruins, were sooted and flame-streaked.

Rye did not halt. He'd seen enough, and simply cutting the chestnut about, started to leave the yard. A harsh command coming from the nearby brush brought him to a stop.

"I'm going to kill you, Rye! Get down off that horse!"

It was the voice of Joe Dix.

CHAPTER XXII

Rigid, the marshal delayed, waiting out the suddenly taut moments. He could not see Dix. The man was somewhere to his left and behind him, well concealed in the tall brush.

"Surprises me some finding you here," Rye said, finally breaking the hush. "Figured you'd be in Trinidad by now."

"Don't you go trying to push me off with your easy talking!" Dix shouted wildly. "Now, you coming off that horse or you want me to shoot you where you are?"

Rye shrugged. Dropping a hand onto the saddlehorn, he swung down. As his heels hit the ground, he pivoted. Dix was still hidden in the dense growth.

"We got Harry Wilse and his bunch," Rye said, striving to distract the man with conversation.

"That was what you come here for, wasn't it?" Joe snapped.

"What you came for, too," Rye said softly. "How about us hashing this over there in the shade of that piñon? Sun's hot."

"Going to be a damned sight hotter where

you're going," Dix declared in a high-pitched tone. "I'm hoping you fry in hell—fry for a thousand years!"

Rye, ignoring the frantic words, crossed to the shadow of the tree he'd mentioned. It could have been a rash move, the marshal knew; considering the unhinged state of mind Joe Dix was in, the slightest thing could set him off, but Rye was gambling on holding the lawman's attention long enough to put himself in a position to use his weapon if talk failed and it became necessary.

Shoot Joe Dix? Kill him? The possibility entered John Rye's mind. He'd cut down on more than his share of outlaws and thought little of it—but a friend?

Rye reached the piñon tree and halted beside it. At that moment he saw Dix. The man was standing back in the oak and mahogany brush, partly hidden by a large rock. The sun was on him full strength, and sweat gleamed on his face, neck, and the backs of his hands. A wildness filled his eyes, the pistol he held was leveled, cocked, needing only the lightest pressure on its trigger to set it off.

"Cooler over here," the marshal said.

Dix frowned, and brushed at his lips. They looked dry, cracked. "You're acting mighty uncaring for somebody that's about to draw his time," Dix said suspiciously.

John Rye's shoulders lifted, then fell resignedly. "I've been there before, Joe, same as you have. You get sort of used to it—and I figure I might as well be comfortable."

Dix mulled that over, edged slowly out from behind the rock and through the brush, and moved into the shade. He was careful, however, to keep a safe distance from the marshal.

"Hot, all right," he conceded, but he was trembling visibly as if having a chill, and his skin beneath its coating of sweat was pale.

"Hot like this riding to Trinidad?" Rye asked, casually.

He was eyeing Dix narrowly, searching for an opening that would afford him a small moment of time in which he could act, disarm the man, but facing a cocked pistol being held unsteadily by one whose mind had snapped promised only uncertain opportunities.

"Never went to Trinidad," Dix mumbled, mopping at his forehead with a free hand. "Started. Got to thinking about what you done to Ruby and turned back."

Rye had avoided speaking of Dix's wife, fearing that mention of her name would further excite him. But it was out now, and there no longer was need for caution.

"I'm saying again I'm sorry about her. I don't think Harry meant to shoot her—just happened she got in the way. It was an accident."

"Wasn't him—it was you!" Dix shouted angrily. "I seen how it was!"

"You couldn't have, not from where you were. It just might've looked like it was me." Rye paused and shook his head. "Joe, you know damn well I'd be more careful than that."

"Like hell you would! All you was wanting was to cut down Harry Wilse any way you could! That's all anything means to you—getting some lousy job done—catching and killing some goddamn outlaw—and you don't care who you tromp on doing it!"

"It was an accident," Rye repeated firmly, endeavoring to break through the wall imprisoning Dix's mind, "And it was Harry Wilse's bullet, not mine."

"I know what I seen," the lawman said, stubbornly.

Rye was silent for a few moments. "How was T.J.? He hurt bad?"

Dix stirred impatiently. "Reckon he's all right. Had to buffalo him when he tried to stop me—"

The marshal frowned. "You clubbed Yocum? Why?"

"He tried stopping me when I decided to come back. Didn't hit him hard—only enough to make him let go."

"Gannon have any other trouble?"

"No—"

"They tell you about Jubilee and Bob Shuster?"

"Yeh."

"Frank Pace's dead, too," Rye said, slowly pulling himself more erect. "He was with me when we caught up with Harry and the rest."

"I heard them cussing Pace. Said he was the reason Jubilee and Shuster got cashed."

Dix seemed to be settling down. His actions were less erratic and his voice had leveled off, but the wildness was still in his eyes.

"Could be. Saved my neck, though. Jack Kincaid threw down on me, had me dead to rights. Frank was laying over in the brush dying—that *vaquero*, Berino, caught him sneaking up and gut shot him. Frank pulled himself together long enough to put a bullet into Kincaid."

"You always was one to ride on high luck—"

"I can say the same for you, Joe. You and me—"

"You ain't horsing me none, Rye!" Dix cut in suddenly, his manner again changing. "I savvy what you're up to, but I ain't swallowing it. You're paying for what you done to Ruby, and us being friends once don't change nothing!"

"Killing me's not going to bring her back—"

A bit at a time, John Rye had been lowering his hand, allowing it to ease toward the weapon on his hip. So far Joe hadn't noticed. Whether—if—he could get in a position to draw and be able to pull and shoot before Dix could react and fire was anybody's guess, but it was beginning to look as if it would be his only chance.

"Maybe it won't, but I'll be making things up to her."

"That's damn fool talk, Joe. Nobody ever squares up anything by killing—they just satisfy themselves. How about holstering that iron and us setting down and talking things over? I can take a stick and do some drawing right here in the sand and show you how it was Ruby got shot—"

Dix was wagging his head slowly. "You ain't talking me out of it, Marshal. I come back here to kill you, and I aim to do it."

Rye's hand froze, still an inch or two from his weapon. He'd best wait a few minutes. "How long you been here?" he asked.

Dix's shoulders stirred. "I don't know—all night, I reckon. I knew you'd be coming."

"How? I told Gannon and T.J. I'd see them in Trinidad."

"It didn't need telling. You never was one to trust somebody else to do something. I knew you'd come back here to see for certain the place had been burned down like you wanted."

Again Joe Dix appeared to be relaxing somewhat, although the hand that gripped the cocked pistol was no lower. But a weariness seemed to be creeping over the man. Rye considered him thoughtfully, concluding that the odds that he could draw and shoot before Dix triggered his .45 might be improving slightly. If he were to survive, however, he'd need to better them even more, and he just might accomplish that by rocking suddenly to one side, thereby destroying Joe's dead-center aim, and hopefully ending up with less than a mortal wound.

But he had to be certain of his own accuracy—of his willingness to shoot. He must kill Joe Dix with his first bullet, for under such circumstances there would be no second try. Kill Joe Dix—a heaviness filled Rye as the thought established itself firmly in his mind. Earlier it had come to him; now, as the inevitable need drew nearer, it struck him forcibly.

How can you kill a respected friend, one of long standing, one grieving over a loss that he is blaming on you but who, in an irrational state of mind, cannot be convinced that he is wrong? John Rye faced the vexing question, thrashing it about in his head, struggling to come up with a different solution.

A sly expression had crossed Joe Dix's sweaty features. "You snaking your hand down to pull that gun you're wearing, Marshal? You damn fool enough to try and out shoot me while I've got the drop on you?"

"I'll try, Joe—you know that. Still think we ought to sit down, talk this over—"

"Hell with that!" Dix suddenly yelled. "We done talked too much! I'm going to blow your head off!"

Rye stiffened. The moment of decision had come.

CHAPTER XXIII

Rye lunged to one side, drew—and fired. In that same fragment of time Dix's gun exploded, seemingly in his face. The shocking impact of a bullet drove him back into the resisting branches of the piñon.

"Ruby!"

He heard Dix's despairing cry as, blinded by the flash, Rye rocked forward and went to his knees, a numbness claiming his left arm and shoulder. Stunned, he shook his head and cleared his senses. A low curse slipped from his dry lips. Joe Dix lay sprawled on the ground a few feet away. A stain of blood was spreading over his chest. There was no need to look close to see if he was dead. Rye became conscious next of the quick pound of hoofs, of a shout, of someone running up to him. He dragged himself erect and turned slowly. It was Hugh Gannon.

"What the hell happened?" the Texan asked, staring at Dix.

165

"Happened?" John Rye echoed bitterly. "I just killed a friend."

"Reckon he about got you, too," Gannon said, glancing at the marshal's shoulder, limp and bleeding. "Why?"

"He got it in his head that I shot his wife. Was Harry Wilse."

Hugh Gannon nodded. "That's what was chawing on him. He took a crazy notion to pull out on us yesterday and come back here. Been sort of loco ever since we started. That bullet that creased him done it, I expect.

"T.J. tried to stop him, got hisself knocked off the saddle for his pains. He's in pretty bad shape, maybe ain't going to make it. Soon as I turned the prisoners over to that sheriff in Trinidad, I lit out for here, hunting him. I was over on the other side of the place when I heard the shooting. We better be getting you to the doc."

"Sure," the marshal murmured, and raising the pistol in his hand, studied it for a long moment. "There's times," he added wearily, "when I hate this goddamn job. This is one of them. Let's load up and get out of here."

Big Bestsellers from SIGNET

☐ **KID ANDREW CODY AND JULIE SPARROW** by Tony Curtis. (#E8010—$2.25)

☐ **WINTER FIRE** by Susannah Leigh. (#E8011—$2.25)

☐ **THE MESSENGER** by Mona Williams. (#J8012—$1.95)

☐ **LOVING SOMEONE GAY** by Don Clark. (#J8013—$1.95)

☐ **HOW TO SAVE YOUR OWN LIFE** by Erica Jong. (#E7959—$2.50)

☐ **FEAR OF FLYING** by Erica Jong. (#E7970—$2.25)

☐ **WHITEY AND MICKEY** by Whitey Ford, Mickey Mantle and Joseph Durso. (#J7963—$1.95)

☐ **MISTRESS OF DESIRE** by Rochelle Larkin. (#E7964—$2.25)

☐ **THE QUEEN AND THE GYPSY** by Constance Heaven. (#J7965—$1.95)

☐ **TORCH SONG** by Anne Roiphe. (#J7901—$1.95)

☐ **OPERATION URANIUM SHIP** by Dennis Eisenberg, Eli Landau and Menahem Portugali. (#E8001—$1.75)

☐ **NIXON VS. NIXON** by David Abrahamsen. (#E7902—$2.25)

☐ **ISLAND OF THE WINDS** by Athena Dallas-Damis. (#J7905—$1.95)

☐ **THE SHINING** by Stephen King. (#E7872—$2.50)

☐ **OAKHURST** by Walter Reed Johnson. (#J7874—$1.95)

THE NEW AMERICAN LIBRARY, INC.,
P.O. Box 999, Bergenfield, New Jersey 07621

Please send me the SIGNET BOOKS I have checked above. I am enclosing $_____(check or money order—no currency or C.O.D.'s). Please include the list price plus 35¢ a copy to cover handling and mailing costs. (Prices and numbers are subject to change without notice.)

Name_____

Address_____

City_____State_____Zip Code_____
Allow at least 4 weeks for delivery

More Big Bestsellers from SIGNET

☐ **FRENCH KISS by Mark Logan.** (#J7876—$1.95)

☐ **COMA by Robin Cook.** (#E7881—$2.50)

☐ **MISTRESS OF DARKNESS by Christopher Nicole.**
(#J7782—$1.95)

☐ **SOHO SQUARE by Clare Rayner.** (#J7783—$1.95)

☐ **DESIRES OF THY HEART by Joan Carroll Cruz.**
(#J7738—$1.95)

☐ **CALDO LARGO by Earl Thompson.** (#E7737—$2.25)

☐ **A GARDEN OF SAND by Earl Thompson.**
(#E8039—$2.50)

☐ **TATTOO by Earl Thompson.** (#E8038—$2.50)

☐ **THE ACCURSED by Paul Boorstin.** (#E7745—$1.75)

☐ **RUNNING AWAY by Charlotte Vale Allen.**
(#E7740—$1.75)

☐ **THE RICH ARE WITH YOU ALWAYS by Malcolm Mac-
donald.** (#E7682—$2.25)

☐ **THE WORLD FROM ROUGH STONES by Malcolm Mac-
donald.** (#J6891—$1.95)

☐ **THE FRENCH BRIDE by Evelyn Anthony.**
(#J7683—$1.95)

☐ **TELL ME EVERYTHING by Marie Brenner.**
(#J7685—$1.95)

☐ **ALYX by Lolah Burford.** (#J7640—$1.95)